P9-DVO-167

A Summer in São Paulo

*These medics are leaving their hearts
in South America!*

Invited to spend the summer in the high-tech,
high-stakes world of São Paulo's premiere teaching
hospital, Hospital Universitário Paulista, it's the
chance for these visiting medical professionals to
shake off their everyday routine—and embrace the
vivacity of South America!

While they're certainly turning up the heat during
the long working days, the warm days and sultry
nights are the perfect setting for romance...
And none of them can resist the call of passion
in paradise!

Discover more in

Awakened by Her Brooding Brazilian
by Ann McIntosh

Falling for the Single Dad Surgeon
by Charlotte Hawkes

Available now!

One Hot Night with Dr. Cardoza
by Tina Beckett

Coming next month!

Dear Reader,

I'm fascinated by how past experiences can inform the present and mold our characters. It's also interesting to see how people can overcome trauma to find a fuller, more satisfying life. That's one of the main themes in *Awakened by Her Brooding Brazilian*.

Both Krysta, a woman dedicated to her work, to the exclusion of all else, and Francisco, a man burned by love, have to find a way to get beyond all they've gone through, so as to find a way to happiness. This is a story of opposites attracting and seeing something beautiful in each other—not with their eyes, but with their hearts!

With a setting like gorgeous Brazil, I think it would be difficult not to fall in love, and I hope you enjoy not only *Awakened by Her Brooding Brazilian*, but all the stories in the series, A Summer in São Paulo.

Regards,

Ann McIntosh

AWAKENED BY HER BROODING BRAZILIAN

———

ANN McINTOSH

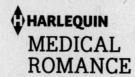

HARLEQUIN

MEDICAL ROMANCE

If you purchased this book without a cover you should be aware
that this book is stolen property. It was reported as "unsold and
destroyed" to the publisher, and neither the author nor the
publisher has received any payment for this "stripped book."

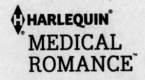

Recycling programs
for this product may
not exist in your area.

ISBN-13: 978-1-335-14939-8

Awakened by Her Brooding Brazilian

Copyright © 2020 by Ann McIntosh

All rights reserved. No part of this book may be used or reproduced in
any manner whatsoever without written permission except in the case of
brief quotations embodied in critical articles and reviews.

This is a work of fiction. Names, characters, places and incidents
are either the product of the author's imagination or are used fictitiously.
Any resemblance to actual persons, living or dead, businesses,
companies, events or locales is entirely coincidental.

This edition published by arrangement with Harlequin Books S.A.

For questions and comments about the quality of this book,
please contact us at CustomerService@Harlequin.com.

Harlequin Enterprises ULC
22 Adelaide St. West, 40th Floor
Toronto, Ontario M5H 4E3, Canada
www.Harlequin.com

Printed in U.S.A.

Ann McIntosh was born in the tropics, lived in the frozen north for a number of years and now resides in sunny central Florida with her husband. She's a proud mama to three grown children, loves tea, crafting, animals (except reptiles!), bacon and the ocean. She believes in the power of romance to heal, inspire and provide hope in our complex world.

Books by Ann McIntosh

Harlequin Medical Romance

The Nurse's Pregnancy Miracle
The Surgeon's One Night to Forever
Surgeon Prince, Cinderella Bride
The Nurse's Christmas Temptation

Visit the Author Profile page at Harlequin.com.

To all the women and young girls dedicated to STEM subjects and the advancement of science. Thank you for your brilliance!

**Praise for
Ann McIntosh**

"This is a beautifully written story filled with all of the feels for a wonderful romance...this one is a real page turner, one that I highly recommend. I really enjoyed this story, it is so very moving as well as being a sensual journey to a HEA...."

— *Goodreads* on
The Surgeon's One Night to Forever

CHAPTER ONE

IF THERE WAS one thing beyond his medical specialty of plastic surgery that Dr. Francisco Carvalho knew, it was fashion, and Dr. Krysta Simpson's formal attire made him almost want to cry.

It was not that it was cheap looking. On the contrary, she'd probably paid a pretty penny for the gown, and the design of the dress, with soft draping at the neckline and cinched waist, was impeccable.

No. He could find no fault with the gown itself, even if it were outdated, but on Dr. Simpson it was a micron away from being an abomination.

Firstly, it was at least one size too big, and hung on her like a sack. Secondly, the celadon silk washed out her complexion—which was toasty brown with rich coppery undertones and freckles—making her look sallow.

To cap it all, her shoes would be more suitable for a woman three times her age, with fallen arches and an abiding distain for anything feminine or fashionable.

Who wore clunky flats with a formal dress?

Apparently, Dr. Simpson did.

It didn't help that she was standing beside a beautiful woman wearing a lovely, infinitely flattering teal, one-shouldered gown. Francisco didn't recognize her, and figured she must be another of the foreign specialists. On her other side was Dr. Flávia Maura, a well-respected researcher into the use of snake and spider venom to treat cancer and other diseases. He'd been surprised when she walked in, since she was in a gorgeous, shimmering green dress, and he'd never seen her in anything other than cargo pants, boots and a T-shirt. She looked fashionable and glamorous, especially in contrast to Krysta Simpson.

Yet, Francisco couldn't help admiring Dr. Simpson's aplomb. She was chatting away with all the insouciance of a woman wearing a bespoke haute-couture outfit, completely unaware of the way she stuck out in the stylishly dressed crowd.

And who could blame her for her confidence? In Francisco's mind, she was a medical goddess of sorts. Not even thirty years old and already a leader in her combined fields of otolaryngology and facial reconstruction, Dr. Krysta Simpson had been making waves in the medical community for the last five years. More if you considered the fact that she was the youngest woman to graduate medical school with those particular specialties. When she'd been picked to work on one of the finest facial transplant teams in the world, no one who'd followed her career was surprised. Her research papers were must-reads in the plastic surgery community, if one wanted to keep current, learn about new techniques and get a feel for what was coming in the future.

After hearing her give a talk at a symposium in Lisbon three years ago, Francisco's one wish had been to speak to her and pick her brain further. When she'd quietly slipped away from the conference and he'd missed that chance, his disappointment had been acute. So, on hearing she was traveling to São Paulo as part of Hospital Universitário Paulista's summer lecture program, he'd hardly believed his luck.

Even more exciting was hearing she'd be performing a mandibular reconstruction on the Brazilian billionaire, Enzo Dos Santos, while there, and Francisco being pegged to assist. Being able to see her in action in theater would be the highlight of his career.

He'd been waiting for a chance to approach her since the welcoming soiree started, but was reluctant to interrupt her conversation. Instead of simply marching over there, he'd been casually circling, inching closer in the crowd. If he wasn't careful, the cocktail portion of the evening would come to a close without him even introducing himself.

He was only about five feet away from her now. Sipping the sparkling water he'd gotten from a waiter, he considered how best to approach. It was testament to how much he'd changed over the last few years. In the past, there'd be no hesitation. That younger Francisco had been supremely sure of himself and his place in the world he inhabited, even though much of that bravado was ill deserved, and had caused more problems than anything else.

The older, wiser man was more watchful, wary. All too cognizant of the way people could misconstrue and misinterpret the most innocent or casual action. The last thing he needed was for her to think he was kissing up to her.

It may have been years since the end of his engagement to Mari, but the unfairness of how he'd been treated by the press, and by people he'd thought of as friends, still stung.

It had left him isolated, and unwilling to open himself up to others, for fear of being betrayed again.

Leaving Rio had felt like making a fresh start, but unfortunately his was a face, and a name, all too recognizable. His problems had followed him to São Paulo like a phantasm that had decided to haunt him forever. Luckily, work kept him busy and gave him little time to stew on the way his life had turned out. And now, getting to work with Dr. Simpson gave him something tangible to look forward to.

Ah, there. Flávia Maura was walking away, and the woman in the teal dress put her hand on Krysta Simpson's arm, seemingly to take her leave as well. As she stepped away in Flávia's wake, and Francisco was about to move toward where Dr. Simpson still stood, he heard the distinctive, dismissive voice of Dr. Silvio Delgado, oncologist.

"The hospital should be more careful of their reputation. First they hire the crazy *selvagem* woman, then the gigolo, and to add insult to injury, they then bring some frump in to lecture. This one looks like a street person."

Francisco's fingers twitched as he reined in the impulse to plant his fist in the other man's face. The situation's only saving grace, in his estimation, was that Delgado spoke in Portuguese, the comment aimed squarely at Francisco and Flávia, rather than Dr. Simpson. The chances of the visiting doctors understanding the nasty comments were slim.

Even as he had the thought, he saw Flávia stop and look back, her brows coming together in a scowl, no doubt at being called a "jungle woman," and Krysta Simpson turned, too, her dark eyes zeroing in on Delgado. Francisco's heart sank momentarily, thinking Dr. Simpson actually knew what was said, but there was no hurt or anger on her face, just curiosity.

When Francisco had first starting modeling at the age of fifteen, his manager and mentor, Caro, had told him, "You must practice different looks, Cisco, so you are always ready to give the photographers exactly what they want. Remember, there are no words to tell the viewer what they should feel. The only clue is in your appearance."

He'd heeded her, of course. The money he made with his face and body was the only way he could achieve his dream of being a doctor. It had felt silly at the time, but he'd done as she'd asked, and developed a repertoire of expressions hailed as impressive.

Now, he put that art to good use.

He turned his head and, as expected, found Delgado's beady, malicious gaze trained on him. Looking down his nose at the shorter man, he met that stare squarely, and allowed his face to fall into an expression of such hauteur he might well have been a king.

You are a worm.

Uncouth.

Dust beneath my feet.

Unworthy of even a moment's more consideration.

All this and worse his expression said, and he saw the exact moment Delgado read it aright. Red washed the other man's face, his nostrils flared slightly and his lips all but disappeared as he pressed them together.

Then Francisco slowly turned his head away, knowing the gesture to be the final insulting blow to the man who felt himself above anyone not from his social circle.

The circle Mari was born into, and Francisco had walked away from, knowing it wasn't anywhere he belonged. Or wanted to belong.

There was a muffled curse from Delgado's direction, a titter from someone else in the vicinity, but Francisco paid neither any mind.

Instead, he walked purposefully toward

Dr. Simpson, releasing his irritation along with a long, silent exhale through his nose.

Working with Dr. Simpson was a once in a lifetime opportunity, and he'd allow nothing—no one—to interfere with it.

Krysta knew herself to be an overachiever, no matter what intellectual journey she embarked on, a trait her therapist had suggested, ad nauseam, she try to dial back. There'd been no reason to immerse herself in learning Portuguese over the last six months since she'd agreed to come to Brazil, but in her mind, there was also no reason *not* to.

It wasn't as though she had a life outside of work—another issue her therapist encouraged her to try to change.

Now, she was glad she'd turned what one colleague had called her "diabolical focus" on learning the language. Being able to understand what was being said, especially when others didn't know you could, was a handy thing indeed.

While she couldn't understand all of the words, she surmised some of them were aimed at the way she was dressed. She was used to it, and whenever she got a strange look or overheard a comment, it rolled right off her.

There were many things in life she really didn't give a fig about. While she could admire other people's clothes sense, or even beautiful tropical decor like that of the room they were in, it was in a distant, disinterested way. She never became emotionally involved with, nor was she particularly moved by, beauty. She'd stood in the Sistine Chapel and thought more about how the painting had been achieved than about how lovely it was.

And that disinterest carried over to her wardrobe.

The dress she was wearing had been bought in London five years before, when she'd suddenly realized she had nothing to wear to a formal dinner. She'd asked the concierge at the hotel for the name of a boutique, gone there, walked in and grabbed the first dress she'd seen. That had caused considerable consternation among the staff, who'd wanted to advise her or, at the very least, force her to try it on.

Krysta had refused, pulling out her card to pay for it. The woman behind the counter had looked as though she might cry, but valiantly tried one more delaying tactic.

Would madam like a pair of shoes to go with the gown?

No, madam would not.

Not when every pair of shoes she saw scattered about the store had sky-high heels!

So, being ridiculed for her appearance meant less than nothing to her. In fact, there was benefit to looking frumpy. Others took you seriously, rather than focusing on your figure, or the fact you were female. The only area of life that mattered was her work: the research and surgeries she undertook in hopes of helping some of those who needed it.

Those things took all the emotional energy she had to expend.

On top of that, even if she were inclined to take umbrage, there was no mistaking the true target of the comments was the tall, exceedingly handsome fellow the other man had been sneering at. The same man striding across the floor toward her. She believed he'd been referred to as a gigolo...

And his reaction had been *amazing*.

Everyone, doctors in particular, had a look they gave those who were being especially displeasing, dense or obstructionist. Krysta's included a deadpan stare and lifted eyebrow, which usually was effective. But she'd never, ever seen such a steely, arrogant expression of distaste on anyone's face before.

How she wished she could pull that off, the next time someone crossed her!

Then there was no more time for rumination, since the man in question came to an abrupt halt in front of her, surprising her no end, since she'd thought he'd go straight by. She found herself looking up into a strong, almost lupine face with intent light brown eyes, and a *zing* of awareness fired down her spine. Even she, no expert on attractiveness, instinctively knew this man would turn every head wherever he went.

He certainly seemed able to turn hers.

"Dr. Simpson." It wasn't a question, so Krysta just looked up at him silently, noting the steely expression wasn't gone from his gaze, but was merely muted. "My name is Dr. Francisco Carvalho, and it's my great pleasure to meet you."

His deep, accented tones seemed to vibrate into her bones in the most surprising way, but she smiled politely as they shook hands, recognizing the name. He was one of the craniofacial surgeons she'd be working with, but he'd missed the video conference calls they'd had regarding the Dos Santos case. It would have been nice to have warning of his attractiveness before this!

"Nice to meet you, too, Dr. Carvalho."

"I am a great fan of yours," he said. "I saw you in Lisbon, speaking about the use of titanium in three-dimensional printing for facial reconstruction, and had hoped to speak more with you after the lecture. I also recently read, with great interest, your paper on the development of new, lighter polymers for the same purpose."

Now there was a shocker.

"But that paper was released only a couple of days ago."

He shrugged lightly, the tiniest of smiles tipping his lips momentarily. Krysta's heart did a weird, crazy little dip as she noted the way his face softened, even as the wolflike appeal increased.

"Anyone in my line of work who has any sense in his or her head knows that when Dr. Krysta Simpson releases a paper, it is in our best interest to read it, as soon as possible."

Normally, compliments and flattery mattered to her as little as clothes or interior design, but something about his tone said that his words were neither. That Dr. Carvalho was stating what was, to him, a fact, and despite herself, Krysta was pleased by it.

Yet it wasn't in her nature to agree.

"I would think Ferguson or Charpentier would be at the top of the must-read list."

Dr. Carvalho nodded. "*Verdade*. Indeed. But they are, in my opinion, old school in their presentations. You take a more progressive line, allowing us a glimpse into what might be, should research advance sufficiently."

Krysta tilted her head briefly to the side in both acknowledgment of the statement and amusement. "I've been taken to task for 'prognosticating' a number of times."

His expression morphed into arrogant amusement in the blink of an eye. "Yet the journals keep printing your papers, and your demand grows. The last I heard, the French team was trying to woo you away from your current position."

"Mere rumor," she replied, although there had been some overtures. "You shouldn't pay attention to gossip."

He looked anything but chastened. In fact, he smiled. "I would like it very much if we sat together at dinner." He gestured to the empty glass in her hand. "May I get you another drink in the meantime?"

"Yes, thank you. I'm having fruit punch—mango and passion fruit, I think the bartender said."

Taking her glass, he stepped away with a murmured, "I'll return in a moment."

Krysta saw the way others watched him walk across to the bar, amused at how right she'd been. Dr. Francisco Carvalho certainly attracted a lot of attention, from admiring stares to what appeared to be envious ones.

"Dr. Simpson, what pleasure it gave me to learn you would be joining us here at the hospital." Krysta turned to see the man who'd made the nasty comment earlier standing behind her, a sly smile on his lips. "I am Dr. Silvio Delgado, oncologist."

She didn't smile back, but shook his outstretched hand and said, "Dr. Delgado."

Not being pleased to make his acquaintance, she didn't say she was.

"You may not know it, but my grandfather was one of the founding contributors to this hospital," he started, obviously expecting her to be overcome with fascination at this information.

Blah, blah, blah...

She tuned him out, wondering if her assistant back in New York had had any luck accessing the information she'd requested. Her latest research project was due to start as soon as she got back to the States and, without the proper accumulation of data, might be pushed back.

Then she heard Dr. Carvalho's name, and tuned back in.

"...no doubt, but I have to tell you his reputation isn't particularly stellar. He might have been famous as a model, but the way he treated his ex-fiancée is a disgrace."

Krysta held up her hand, cutting the man off. "But is he a good doctor?"

Delgado blinked, several times, rapidly. "I beg your pardon?"

"Does he do his job in an acceptable way? Is he a good surgeon?" she asked, making her voice slow, as though to make sure he understood.

"Well... I... I suppose so," he replied, and she saw the way his ears reddened.

She shrugged. "That's all I care about."

"Your drink, Dr. Simpson."

Speak of the devil.

"Thank you, Dr. Carvalho," she replied, turning to take the frosty glass from his hand. Had he heard the exchange between herself and the other man? There was nothing at all in his expression or demeanor to give her any clue. This Dr. Carvalho was a master at hiding his thoughts, unless and until he wanted to share them.

"It appears dinner is about to be served," he said, extending his arm toward her as an announcement to that effect came over the PA system. "Shall we go through?"

"Yes, thank you," she replied, laying her

fingers on his impressive brachioradialis and strangely having to squelch the urge to squeeze it, just to see if it were as strong as she thought. Then she gave Dr. Delgado a level, straight-faced look and continued, "You will excuse us, won't you? I'm famished."

She saw the exact instant Dr. Delgado realized she'd spoken in Portuguese. His eyes widened, and his face paled. It took everything she had inside not to lose her poker face at his horrified expression.

And she now knew, for a fact, how hard Dr. Carvalho's arm muscle really was, as it tightened to rock beneath her fingers. Glancing up into his startled face, she said, "I hope my accent isn't terrible. I've only been learning the language for a few months."

He blinked, and she saw amusement flood his eyes, causing them to gleam. "Not at all," he replied. "In fact, it is *perfeita*."

CHAPTER TWO

Francisco hurried across the grounds toward the conference and lecture center, glancing at his watch as he went.

Ora bolas! Krysta Simpson's first lecture was supposed to start in less than a minute, and he was only now getting through the door into the building. It had been a busy morning, one that started at 4:00 a.m. with a call from the hospital concerning a victim of a robbery gone wrong; he'd had severe zygomatic and maxillary fractures. They'd taken him straight into surgery, and the delicate procedure of rebuilding his orbital structure hadn't ended until almost nine. Luckily, there didn't appear to be damage to his eye, but ophthalmology had been alerted and a specialist would be along to examine the patient once the swelling had abated.

Francisco had already told his head of department that, whenever time permitted, he wanted to attend as many of Dr. Simpson's lectures as possible, and Dr. Emanuel had readily agreed. Getting her to Paulista's was a coup for the hospital, since it was well-known she rarely lectured, preferring to devote her time to research and major, cutting-edge operations. Having her agree to perform the surgery on Dos Santos, who'd suffered oral cancer, was an added bonus. The patient had had a segment of his mandible removed, along with his tumor, in London, and specifically wanted her to do the reconstruction.

All the team members were familiar with the technique she would be using, where a piece of the patient's fibula, along with blood vessels and a flap of skin, would be used to reconstruct the piece of mandible removed by the oncologist. Francisco had done several, even a couple where the inferior alveolar nerve running through the jaw to the chin and lower lip had been repaired as well. What Krysta Simpson brought to the table was a newer way of approaching the operation itself, and techniques not used everywhere yet.

Beyond all that, though, Francisco found her even more fascinating than he expected. Before meeting her, his sole focus had been on her work, the advances she'd been a part of in the world of facial reconstruction and the research she spearheaded.

That was before he'd heard her cut Delgado off when the other man was trying to poison her against him. And when she'd spoken in almost-perfect Portuguese... If he were still capable of doing so, he would have fallen for her right there and then. It had been *magnifica*. Just the expression on Delgado's face had been enough to elevate the evening into one of the best Francisco had had in years.

They'd sat at the same table at dinner, and spoke almost exclusively to each other during the meal. He'd found himself avidly watching her face as she spoke, all but drowning in the twinkling brown eyes. It was only after he went home that it struck him why he'd enjoyed the night so much.

Communicating with Krysta Simpson had been easy, without any kind of undertones, or nosy questions. He'd been at ease with her, and found the wall of reticence he'd built up over the years rather thinner around her than it usually was. Perhaps it was because of her direct way of speaking, and how obvious it was she didn't care about his storied past. It had been a long time since he'd felt so comfortable with anyone outside of his family, and had been a very pleasant experience.

Although he could certainly do without the thrill of attraction he felt toward her.

Now, finally getting to the lecture hall, he glanced in through the glass at the top of the door and found everyone already seated, with a few people even standing at the sides and back of the room. Most were students and residents, but there were a few established surgeons seated at the front. Not wanting to cause a disturbance when he expected Dr. Simpson to step out onto the stage at any moment, Francisco turned and headed for the door leading to the room adjacent to the hall. It was where lecturers waited for their audience to assemble, but it also led directly to the wings, via a corridor. His plan was to quietly make his way to the edge of the stage, and listen to her from there.

It would cause much less fuss than walking into the crowded room and perhaps even have one of his residents get up to offer him a seat, which was not outside the realm of possibility. All the young doctors he supervised were ambitious, and keen to make a good impression on the more experienced staff members, in hopes of it giving them a leg up on the competition.

The L-shaped waiting area beside the lecture hall was much like any of the green rooms Francisco had been in during his modeling days. There were a few upholstered chairs, a couch, coffee table, refreshment area and, set into a secluded alcove at the back, a desk. At first, when he entered, he thought it empty, then he heard what sounded like low mumbling coming from the desk area. Curiosity took him the steps necessary to peer around the corner, and he was taken aback to find Dr. Simpson standing beside the desk.

Her back was to him, her face to the wall, her hands pressed flat against the surface in front of her, the knuckles almost white with the pressure she was exerting on her fingers.

His first instinct was to leave her alone, but something in the stiffness of her posture, the cadence of her voice as she recited something to herself, kept him there.

"Dr. Simpson…"

She turned a pale, sweat-sheened face to him, snapping, "I asked for just a few more minutes." Then she shook her head, as though trying to bring herself back from whatever unhappy place she'd just been.

"My apologies," he said stiffly, annoyed with himself for disturbing her. "I thought perhaps you were unwell."

"Sick," she mumbled. Then her voice rose. "God, I hate public speaking."

She seemed so confident generally it was startling to see her this way, and he said, "But you do it so well. No one would ever believe your aversion."

Krysta gave him a wan look as she reached into the pocket of her oversize jacket and pulled out a handful of tissues. Dabbing her forehead, she replied, "Do you know why you couldn't find me to speak to me in Lisbon after my presentation? Because I was in the bathroom throwing up. At least this time I threw up first."

When he'd mentioned he'd looked for her then, she hadn't commented. Now he understood why.

"If you hate it so much, why do it?" he asked, honestly perplexed. It wasn't as though she needed to raise her profile in the medical world. And if she did, Brazil probably wouldn't be first on the list of places to do so.

"I'd promised myself not to do it again, but over the last couple of years I've been trying to work through some…issues, and my therapist told me I need to face my fears. And she also told me I needed to get out more, experience more of life, since I spend all my time working. Brazil seemed like a good place to kill two birds with one stone."

Francisco was unsure of what to say to that but, before he could reply, the noise level in the lecture hall seemed to rise to a grumbling murmur. Krysta obviously heard it, too, as she straightened, giving her forehead one last pat down with the tissues. To his amazement, all signs of distress and trepidation fell away from her face, and although he saw her swallow hard once, she appeared perfectly collected, if still a little pale.

"Okay," she said, as much to herself as to him. "I'm ready now."

She walked past him with long confident strides, and then paused to glance back at him. "Are you staying for the lecture?"

He gestured to the corridor she was about to walk down. "I'll be watching from the wings."

The smile she gave him made something warm and pleasant bloom in his chest.

"Good. Great."

"And perhaps we can lunch together afterward?" he asked before she disappeared. "Before I do my rounds?" They were getting together that afternoon for a preliminary team meeting regarding the upcoming surgery, but the urge to spend more time with her was unmistakable.

"Sure," was the nonchalant answer.

Then she was gone, and as he followed and saw her step out onto the stage, the applause began.

There were many divides between Krysta and her father, but as she explained to Dr. Carvalho over lunch, she owed her ability to deal with whatever was happening directly to him.

"He's an auto mechanic," she said as she arranged the food on her plate to her specifications: meat at five o'clock, rice at seven and vegetables taking up the rest of the space. No restaurant, or cafeteria like the one here at the hospital, ever got it quite right. "He proudly calls himself a grease monkey, and never really understood why I wanted to go into medicine, yet everything important I know about getting through life I learned from him."

The conversation had started when Francisco had asked how she'd gone from a shaking mess to composed so quickly. Usually, she'd have brushed it off, embarrassed to be seen that way by anyone, but, somehow, she'd minded neither his intrusion nor the question. She felt remarkably comfortable with Francisco Carvalho, once she subdued the rush of awareness she experienced whenever their eyes met.

Seeing the quizzical expression being sent her way, Krysta elaborated. "He always told us, 'Fear and doubt are contagious. If you let others see you're feeling them, they'll catch it, and mirror it back to you tenfold.' In my head, I equate it to when a family gets the flu, and keep passing it back and forth. When you get it the second time, it's usually much worse."

"Ah," he said, nodding. "I see. So you trained yourself to go through the fear and get the job done."

"You have to sometimes," she agreed, while putting together the perfect forkful of food. "I've gotten out of the habit of pushing myself, outside of my usual work life, but I'm thankful to know that ability to compartmentalize in uncomfortable situations hasn't deserted me."

"I enjoyed your lecture, as I knew I would." He had a direct, unruffled way of speaking she really liked. "The information you're imparting to our staff should prove highly valuable."

She finished chewing and swallowed before she replied. "It's available elsewhere. I just have it put all together in one presentation, because of my research and specialties."

The lecture, the first of three parts, dealt with the ever-widening and exciting world of biomaterials for medical applications. It was a topic she was fascinated by, since new discoveries opened up advanced and improved ways of disease diagnosis, delivery of medications, even tissue generation. In later lectures she'd go into greater detail regarding specific applications, particularly when used for facial reconstruction.

He shook his head, giving her one of his abbreviated smiles.

"The information you have is *not* available to everyone. You must have gotten fifty different permissions just to do this lecture series."

She tried not to smirk, but probably failed. "More like sixty, including being able to talk about and show some of the work that went into the facial transplant I assisted with."

Francisco's eyes widened. "Really?"

"Mmm-hmm," she murmured around another mouthful of food, unreasonably glad to have truly impressed him with that pronouncement. She wasn't sure who at Paulista's pulled the strings, but someone at the hospital had a great deal of clout.

He took a moment to have another bite of his *feijoada*, which reminded her a little of Jamaican stewed peas, although it was made with black beans instead of red kidney beans and had sausage in it, rather than just salted meat. She'd opted for *churrasco* and wasn't disappointed as the tender barbecued beef melted in her mouth, releasing its delicious flavor. Francisco swallowed, and seemed about to say something, when Flávia Maura stopped by their table, tray in hand, and Krysta looked up to smile at the other woman.

"Hi," Flávia said, speaking directly to Krysta after acknowledging Francisco with a terse nod. "I was wondering if you wanted to come over to the sanctuary for a tour sometime while you're here. I can show you the live specimens, and some of the research data I've collected."

An involuntary shiver rustled up Krysta's back.

"I'm really interested in your findings, because I think the possible applications are fascinating, but unfortunately I don't do snakes. Just the thought of being around a lot of them gives me the chills."

"You're not afraid of them, are you?" Flávia seemed both bemused and disappointed. "As a scientist, surely you understand their importance, ecologically and medicinally?" She shook her head, then ran her fingers through her hair. "The amount of time I spend trying to explain that to people…"

"Oh, I understand," Krysta said, not at all offended at being taken to task. She completely related to Flávia's drive and passion. Although their fields were very different, the other woman's intensity mirrored her own. "I've just never been comfortable with reptiles or amphibians, although I don't mind arachnids."

Flávia's gaze swung toward the door and lingered there for a moment. As a hint of color touched the other woman's face, Krysta glanced that way in time to see the British oncologist Jake Cooper heading for the buffet line. When she looked back at Flávia, it was to see the other woman rubbing one cheek, as though to erase the warmth accumulating there. Then her hand dropped away, and she shook her head slightly, her gaze returning to meet Krysta's.

"Well, if you change your mind, let me know. The invitation is always open." Flávia glanced at Francisco, and added, "You can come, too, if you like."

He dipped his head in acknowledgment.

"Thank you for the invitation but, unlike Krysta, I'm leery of spiders, ever since I was bitten by a brown widow as a child."

Flávia made a little sound best described as a snort. "*Latrodectus geometricus.* Did you not check your shoes before putting them on?"

Francisco shook his head, but there was a wry set to his mouth. "More like stuck my hand into somewhere it didn't belong."

Flávia nodded, and gave him a little smile in return. "I've been known to do that myself, from time to time."

Why did Krysta feel there was more to both those stories than met the eye? Her curiosity was definitely piqued. Just as it had been when she noticed how coolly distant Francisco was with everyone. Well, except her.

Then Flávia was taking her leave, striding off to sit at one of the other tables before Krysta even thought to invite her to sit with them.

Francisco gave her one of his noncommittal looks, and said, "I thought you were on a campaign to overcome your fears. Wouldn't this be a good opportunity?"

Was he being serious, snide or teasing? Krysta narrowed her eyes in an attempt to figure it out. Then she noticed the twinkle in his eyes, and decided it was the latter. To date, she'd seen nothing snide in his manner, which was probably why they got along so well. After so many years of, in different situations, being the youngest, or only female, or just plain different, she was adept at spotting even a hint of condescension.

Looking down at her plate, she set about arranging another forkful, and replied, "Perhaps I'll go...if you do."

There. When she glanced up, the twinkle in his eyes had definitely deepened, and his lips quirked in amusement. "Hmm, I wouldn't wait around for that if I were you. I have no problem admitting I avoid spiders whenever I can, and tend to swat the ones I can't elude."

Krysta gave an exaggerated look over her shoulder. "You better not let Flávia hear you say that. You've already moved down a few notches in her estimation, and that would send you straight to Hades, without even a pause in purgatory."

He laughed.

Not just a chuckle, but a full-on deep laugh.

It was such a departure from the contained and controlled Dr. Carvalho, Krysta found herself transfixed by the sight.

The way his face lit up. The low, somehow sexy rumble of his merriment. The crinkling of the skin at the corners of his eyes, and slashes, like long dimples, in his cheeks.

Heat washed through her veins, out into every crevice and corner of her body, the sensation unlike any she'd experienced before. Instinctively, she looked down, not wanting him to catch her staring, and tried to catch her suddenly nonexistent breath.

The sensation was akin to how she felt before lecturing: scared, a little shaky. Completely sure something unknown and horrible was coming her way.

Frazzled, she shoved the fork into her mouth, even though half the salad had fallen off.

She'd have to try to work it out later, although she had the distinct feeling there was some important data she lacked.

His laughter subsided, but there was still a touch of amusement in his voice as he said, "Would you like to do rounds with me, before the meeting with the surgical team?"

No.

Yes.

No.

Indecision wasn't something Krysta tolerated in others, and despised in herself, yet her brain ping-ponged back and forth in a most annoying manner at his simple question. Then common sense reasserted itself.

"Do you have any patients I could be of particular help to? If not, I need to contact my research assistant and make sure everything is under control before he goes on holiday next week."

The smile stayed on his lips, but she thought she saw a flash of disappointment in his eyes as he replied, "No, not really. But I'm sure the residents would have questions they'd love to ask."

Ah, he was thinking about the residents. That made sense. She shrugged, and concentrated on her plate.

"I'll be available for the next few months. There'll be plenty of time for them."

"Indeed," he replied, but something in his voice made her glance up at him, and now it was she who was disappointed when he wasn't looking at her, so she couldn't see his eyes. "Perhaps, if you're not too busy, we could lunch again tomorrow."

"Perhaps," she replied, trying to remain noncommittal, even as she knew she'd be there.

CHAPTER THREE

LATER THAT EVENING, Krysta made her way down to the indoor pool at the apartment building where she was staying. She'd tried to settle in for the evening, but her whirring brain made her restless, and swimming laps was one surefire way to work off some of her excess energy.

All in all, it had been a constructive day, but the stress of lecturing, coupled with the preoperation group meeting, rendered her unable to relax.

Getting to the pool, she was happy to find it deserted. After she'd shed her robe and slippers, she made her way to the deep end, putting on her goggles as she went.

Then she dove in, automatically counting the strokes it took to get to the opposite end, and then keeping count of the laps. But even so occupied, her brain still had more than enough space left over to go through the day once more.

Yet, surprisingly, considering how stressful it had been, it wasn't the lecture or the upcoming operation she found herself contemplating.

It was Francisco Carvalho, and her completely untoward reactions whenever he was around. Those moments of hesitation—procrastination—when he'd invited her to accompany him on rounds was bad enough but, to make it worse, she'd found herself distracted by him during the meeting with the surgical team.

She'd brought one of the three-dimensional replicas of Mr. Dos Santos's skull with her, showing how it had been prior to the segmental mandibulectomy, along with a 3-D model of his mandible, and recent scans.

"The oncological team used fluorescent contrast preop to locate the cancer cells, and luckily, because of that, we have decent margins to work with. As you know, we'll be performing a vascularized fibula flap transfer, with simultaneous dental-implant placement. We will be using titanium plates specifically crafted for Mr. Dos Santos to hold the transferred bone in place, along with cutting templates to shape the fibula into the exact shape needed."

Francisco leaned closer to get a better look at the 3-D skull, bringing his shoulder into close proximity to hers. Warmth flooded her arm, making her wonder if the heat emanated from him or if her body was spontaneously creating it.

Flummoxed, she was forced to strain to concentrate when one of the residents raised his hand and said, "If I may ask, why wasn't the reconstruction done immediately following the mandibulectomy? Isn't that the standard of care?"

Krysta dragged her mind back to the meeting, but it was Jake Cooper who answered.

"Dr. Simpson wasn't available to perform the operation when I had the mandibulectomy scheduled," he replied. "And Mr. Dos Santos insisted she be the one to head the team."

"Dr. Simpson was in France, assisting with a facial transplant," Francisco interjected. "And some of what the French were able to achieve, she will be sharing with us in her lectures."

That brought another little murmur from the assembled group, which Krysta ignored. Just as she outwardly ignored Francisco's interruption, even as she felt a silly little glow of pride.

Instead of acknowledging his words, she continued. "While it is common practice, none of the data show any difference in outcome if the reconstruction is secondary. And since it affords us an opportunity to make full use of the new technology, we can ensure a shorter, more efficient operation, along with superior function and aesthetic results, long-term. In consultation with both Dr. Cooper and the patient, it was decided the benefits of waiting outweighed the detriments."

Francisco asked, "Could you expound on that a little, Dr. Simpson? I'm interested in how that decision was made."

She'd found herself reluctant to look directly at him, so she let her gaze roam the rest of the people in the room.

"Every patient is different," she began, gathering her thoughts carefully. "In situations such as the one Mr. Dos Santos found himself in, each person has their own concerns and fears. Some just want the cancer removed, no matter what that entails, not thinking past surviving. Others fear the surgery almost as much, if not more, than the disease. In this particular case, on speaking to the patient, I realized he wasn't particularly worried about his prognosis. He truly believed his strength of will would make his recovery all but inevitable. But there was one thing he was deeply worried about, and that was his postoperative appearance and facial functionality."

There was a murmur through the room, and Krysta held up her hand to silence it.

"Mr. Dos Santos isn't just a wealthy businessman, but the face of his company, and of his *futebol* team, Chutegol. Much of his success has come from being 'Senhor Chutegol,' recognized by everyone, parlaying that recognition into bigger and better successes."

At the mention of the well-known soccer team, which was in the prestigious Brasíleirão league, the assembled team nodded, and Krysta could see understanding dawning in most of their expressions.

"Once I realized how important the aesthetic result was to him, I then spoke to him about timelines. I explained that if I were to do the reconstruction secondary to the mandibulectomy, I'd want to wait until he'd also finished his radiation treatments, and his recovery time would be extended. He didn't care about that. As most of you know, he'd announced his diagnosis to the media, and was willing to take as long as necessary to recover, as long as he looked almost the same when he finally reemerged. That was when I suggested the CT mapping, and 3-D printing approach.

"And there was one final deciding factor," she continued. "I explained to him that I was committed to coming here for three months, and so would have just a short window prior to my visit to do the surgery. That was when he requested, if possible, that the surgery be done here, in his home country, and be used as a training opportunity."

Once more, murmurs broke out around the room, but there was a decidedly appreciative cadence to them.

"While you all are familiar with the standard fibular free-flap reconstruction, introducing you to some of the newer techniques in presurgical planning, along with the 3-D planned plates and templates, will serve you well in the years to come. It's an exciting and fast-evolving technique in our line of work."

They'd gone on to discuss the operation in detail, but through it all Krysta was supremely aware of Francisco next to her, whether he was contributing to the conversation or not.

Now, as she finished her twenty-fourth lap,

she had to admit to herself the patently obvious truth.

She was attracted to him.

That in itself was unusual enough to throw her off her stride. Not that it was the first time she'd found a man attractive, but unlike the other times, there was a stronger pull, a growing need for his company she didn't understand.

Worse was this sense of wanting to do something about it, take it further to see where it might lead. That was very different from the times before, when she'd been content to look and do nothing about her feelings.

Not that she'd know how to go about getting from point A to point B with a man like Francisco Carvalho.

She'd succumbed to curiosity and looked him up on the internet. Francisco Carvalho had lived an exciting life as a model prior to becoming a surgeon. Back then, he was known as Cisco, and there were myriad pictures of him in ads and on catwalks around the world. He'd even been the face of a cologne produced by a designer whose name even Krysta recognized.

And then there were the shots of him at parties and galas, and in many of them he had a gorgeous blonde woman on his arm, described in some of the captions as Mariella Guzman, his fiancée. That wide-eyed beauty had seemed the perfect complement to Francisco's dark, brooding handsomeness. Recalling Dr. Delgado's comments on the night of the reception, she'd been tempted to see if there were any articles saying what happened, but decided against it. She'd seen enough to tell her everything she needed to know.

Francisco Carvalho may be her contemporary in the medical world, but in every other way, he was light-years beyond her.

All her life she'd been an outsider, far younger than any of her classmates or work contemporaries. When her mental contemporaries had been experimenting with love and sex, she'd been focused on her studies or career. And before she'd gotten to the point where perhaps she'd have been open to exploring her own sexuality, she'd been traumatized by an assault.

That wasn't something she'd thought or talked about in years, pushing it away and minimizing it in her head. After all, she told herself, it wasn't as though she'd been raped. There were other young girls who'd been hurt far more severely than she had.

It wasn't until she'd started seeing Dr. Hellman that she'd begun to see the ramifications. At fourteen, Krysta had learned to repress her sexuality and minimize any outward signs of femininity. Then, safe in the bastion of her denial, she'd decided relationships, even casual ones, weren't in the cards.

Yet, for all the talking and analyzing, she wasn't ready to let go of her disguise, or venture out of the safety zone. Her work still was her be-all and end-all, and she couldn't afford distractions.

Case in point, she thought as she got to the wall in the deep end and hung on, instead of doing a racing turn and continuing. Thinking about Francisco Carvalho had made her lose count of her laps, when usually she could keep track of them effortlessly, even while thinking about other things. If he could so easily shut down a function of her brain, one she considered automatic, what could he do to the rest of it, if she let him?

Yet, she knew he wouldn't be as easy to dismiss from her mind as the other men she'd been attracted to. There was definitely something different about Francisco, something compelling. It wasn't his looks, although she thought him handsome. Looks alone would never be enough to pique her interest.

Treading water, she considered exactly what it was about him that gave her goose bumps, and made her heart race, but couldn't pinpoint any one thing.

That, in itself, was additionally frustrating. Krysta was used to being able to work though almost any puzzle and find a logical solution.

Perhaps you're looking for the answer to the wrong question.

Her therapist's voice sounded in her head, making her wrinkle her nose. It was one of Dr. Hellman's more annoying sayings, especially when she never seemed willing to let on what the right question was. The only statement more annoying was, "You need to step out of your comfort zone."

Well, she had, hadn't she? Agreeing to come to Brazil and lecture. Dr. Hellman had seemed pleased when Krysta had told her about the trip. Of course, she'd also told her to take the opportunity to stretch herself even more. There were, according to the psychologist, so many things Krysta had missed out on growing up. Not because her parents had pushed her, but because Krysta had pushed herself.

Realizing she'd done it not just because she wanted to succeed, but because it was a great way to isolate herself socially and feel safe, had been revelatory.

Shoving back from the wall, she floated

into the middle of the pool, looking up at the ceiling, drifting lazily in the water, rather than cleaving through the way she usually did.

She'd thought she was fine the way she was, but she'd had to reevaluate that supposition. After all, no one had forced her to make that first appointment with Dr. Hellman. It clearly had been something inside her telling her it was time to get things right in her head. Perhaps telling her a full, successful career wasn't all there was in life. Warning that if she didn't make some changes soon, she may be leaving it too late.

"You're a forward-thinking innovator at work," Dr. Hellman had said, her eyes glinting behind her glasses. "Someone who develops new techniques and isn't afraid to move forward boldly into the future. Why not do that in the rest of your life? Isolating yourself, thinking only about work, isn't healthy."

Hearing those words at first made Krysta feel powerful, in control of whatever might happen. But later, alone at home, they'd come back to mind and scared her almost silly. Why they filled her with such trepidation, she hadn't wanted to contemplate.

Perhaps it was because to go down that road would be to have to acknowledge exactly how much she *had* missed out on.

The friendships, like those she'd seen her brothers develop with others, and her parents had nurtured, even when distance divided them from those closest to them.

The family ties, which she'd neglected so badly in the pursuit of excellence, using work as an excuse to avoid the functions and get-togethers others took for granted.

Meaningful relationships, such as the one her parents shared with each other.

Just now, though, it was the putting aside of her sexuality that felt most important.

Apparently, her body thought giving it free rein was long overdue. Just being around Francisco Carvalho brought all her senses to life, arousing sensations she'd never experienced before.

What she was going to do about any of it, she had no idea. But even if she did get brave enough to try to act on these feelings, it would have to wait until after Enzo Dos Santos's surgery.

She wouldn't allow anything, neither Francisco Carvalho nor her own carnal urges, to interfere with her concentration.

Francisco stood under the shower, trying to get the streams of warm water to unravel his knotted muscles. It wasn't that the day had been terribly stressful. Yes, he'd been called out early in the morning, and had another emergency come into the hospital just as he was getting ready to leave, but he was used to that.

What he wasn't used to was Krysta Simpson.

There was an ineffable aura about her that fascinated him intensely. The more time he spent with her, the more captivated he became—with her confidence, precision, razor-sharp mind and the easy way she spoke to everyone, even while maintaining a certain mysterious distance.

Yet, although all those things would be more than enough, Francisco knew himself to be attracted to her physically as well.

More than once, when she was lecturing and in the presurgery meeting, he'd lost track of what she was saying. Not because he wasn't interested, or enthralled by the subject matter, but because he'd caught himself staring at her lips as she spoke, or at the movement of her hands.

Those hands were both capable and surprisingly graceful, and he'd drifted off into a fantasy of what they would feel like on his skin.

Even now, as he was reiterating to himself

just how bad that was, his body reacted to the memory, tightening and hardening against his will.

And it truly wasn't at all a good idea to even entertain any fantasies about Dr. Krysta Simpson, for a number of reasons.

Trying to ignore his burgeoning erection, he silently listed them again.

Krysta Simpson had not, by look or word, expressed the slightest interest in him. She was friendly and professional and, in his estimation, they had a great rapport. But beyond that, he saw nothing to indicate she had any other feelings toward him, and he certainly wasn't the type to push.

Besides, having a months-long affair with someone, who would then quickly disappear, did not appeal to him.

Or certainly *shouldn't*.

Then there was the fact she was a visitor to his country, here to do a job. A colleague whose reputation was stellar, and far above his own. Krysta was a star, world renowned, while Francisco was simply a competent plastic and reconstructive surgeon, good at his job but nothing special. To even spend too much time with her was to court disaster, in the same way being engaged to Mari had caused him untold pain and embarrassment.

All too well could he imagine the whispers, not to mention those, like Delgado, who would say aloud for everyone to hear that he was, once again, trying to sleep his way to success. Using looks and charm to advance into a world where he didn't belong.

He knew the gossip that swirled around him in the hospital, and it made him leery of doing anything to stir the pot. Getting too close to Krysta Simpson definitely would do that.

The thought chilled him, and thankfully his ardor waned. Turning off the water, he stepped out of the shower to grab a towel.

He'd been burned by others' cruelty and lies before, and had no intention of doing anything to precipitate that again.

Instead, he needed to remind himself of how far he'd come, how hard he'd worked to get to where he was. Others could say modeling was easy, or believe the lies told about him—that he'd used his association with Mari to further himself—but he knew the truth. It had been a long, backbreaking and often lonely road he'd taken, and there'd been times he'd wanted to quit, to go home to his family and childhood friends. Only his dream of becoming a doctor had kept him there, working and studying in equal measure.

When he'd met Mari and fallen for her, he'd thought life could get no better. By then he was almost finished medical school, and hadn't cared that she came from a wealthy family. Foolishly, he'd thought it didn't matter. He knew he'd be able to support them, between what he'd had saved and what he would earn as a surgeon. What he hadn't taken into consideration was the different rules by which the privileged lived, where they would steamroll over anyone to get what they wanted, or to get out of trouble.

But he'd learned it the hard way, and discovered it was best not to give yourself too freely, because it opened you up to having what you'd said, done or felt used against you. He'd paid dearly for allowing Mari into his heart, and it wasn't an experience he wanted to go through again.

CHAPTER FOUR

HER DAYS FELL into a routine, which normally would have pleased her, but Krysta grew increasingly restive. It wasn't just that she was used to being far busier, since there was actually quite a bit of research she could, and did, do via computer. Even with the upcoming operation, slated for the following week, there just wasn't enough to fill her time, or quell her almost constant disquiet.

It didn't help that, when at the hospital, she was in almost constant contact with Francisco.

His friendly demeanor had cooled somewhat, though. They still had lunch together, and she did afternoon rounds with him, as well as meeting with the surgical team often, but the connection they'd developed in the first few days seemed to wane. There were no questions now about her family or anything else, other than work.

She should have been happy about that, since it afforded her an opportunity to put her own silly attraction into perspective. Instead, it just made her wonder what had happened to cause his withdrawal. If she had more courage, she'd ask, but while she was willing to do or ask anything in a medical setting to get the answers she needed, in social situations she hadn't a clue.

Sometimes, when he wasn't expecting it, she'd glance his way, only to find him concentrating intently on her face. In those moments, as their gazes collided, the gleam in his eyes threw her usually focused brain into disarray, and the warmth flooding her system made her want to squirm.

It was disturbing on so many levels, she thought as she was on her way to the director's office. Stabbing the elevator button with unnecessary force brought her no relief.

"Hey. What did that button ever do to you?"

The question, laden with amusement, had Krysta turning, a smile already in place.

"Flávia, don't you see the sheer cheek of it? Its perfection aggravates me."

Flávia laughed with her, but there was a little edge to it. "Yes," she replied, and now there was no mistaking the acerbic tone.

"Perfection is definitely annoying. How are things going?"

"Very well," Krysta replied, perhaps not completely honestly. "I know how silly it sounds, but I'm surprised at how fast paced everything is here."

Flávia shrugged. "Hospitals and cities are mostly the same everywhere, aren't they? Way too many people for my liking."

Krysta chuckled, glancing around and seeing Amy Woodell coming in through the front doors. She waved to get the approaching woman's attention, curious to hear how the other woman was getting on. They'd met on arrival in Brazil, in the immigration line at the airport, and spent some time chatting at the welcome reception. But because of being in different departments, they hadn't seen each other since.

As Amy came up, Krysta thought she looked weary. Maybe even frazzled.

"I think I'm having a case of déjà vu," Amy said as she got to where they were standing. "Only, I wasn't this tired at the welcome party."

"We were just talking about how fast paced everything is here in São Paulo," Krysta replied.

Amy nodded, then asked, "Did you already

do your seminars? I haven't even looked at the lineup yet."

"No," Flávia replied.

"I've done the first of mine," Krysta said. "One down, two to go."

She glanced at the elevator panel, seeing that the one she wanted was still on the top floor, while another was approaching.

"Which floor are you headed to?"

"Fourth. I'm meeting Roque Cardoza," Amy answered, with a little scowl.

"Is he the one you were sitting by at the party?"

"Yep. He's in charge of me for the next couple of weeks. I have to do anything he says, evidently."

Flávia's head swiveled toward Amy while Krysta raised her eyebrows, fighting the smile she could feel tugging at her lips.

"I mean related to the job," Amy interjected quickly, making Krysta chuckle.

"Com certeza. Só o trabalho."

Flávia's voice had a touch of mirth in it too, letting Krysta know she wasn't the only one who'd found Amy's choice of words amusing.

"It's not like he's hard to look at. If that's your thing."

A rush of rosy color flowed up Amy's face until her cheeks glowed. "You guys… I don't think of him like that at all. Besides, he's really *not* all that good-looking."

As the two elevators Amy and Flávia were waiting for arrived, and the three women took their leave of each other, Krysta saw the man in question step into the car behind Amy.

Had he heard their conversation? She rather hoped not. But as she stepped into the elevator going up to the executive floor she turned her thoughts back to her own dilemma.

What to do about Francisco Carvalho…?

The director welcomed Krysta into his office and fussed about for a few minutes, offering coffee, tea or water, making sure she was comfortably situated in one of the cushioned visitor's chairs. Then he sat forward, placing his crossed arms on his desk, and smiled.

"I hope everything at the hospital is to your specifications, Dr. Simpson?"

Despite the pleasant expression on his face, she thought his eyes seemed watchful, and she knew he was worried she'd come to complain about something, or someone. She smiled back at him.

"Paulista's is wonderful, Dr. Andrade. You know it is. State-of-the-art equipment, and wonderfully trained, professional staff. What could I possibly find lacking?"

He sat back, clearly pleased with her little outpouring of sugar, and his smile widened. "So, what can I do for you, then?"

"I heard one of your residents talking about a planned surgical clinic, and wanted to offer my services. It is slated for my final month here, isn't it?"

Hearing about the clinic hadn't been the only draw. She'd also gotten a peek at the roster, and realized Francisco's name wasn't on it.

Dr. Andrade's brow furrowed slightly, even as he nodded. "Yes, but it will not be held here in the hospital, but in Aparecida, which is about two hours northeast."

She shrugged. "I don't mind traveling to participate. It will give me a chance to get to see a bit more of your beautiful country."

Still, he looked concerned. "I doubt there will be anything on the surgical roster that falls in with your specialty, Dr. Simpson."

"Oh, I'm not expecting facial transplants, or anything like that, but it was my understanding that there would be a number of cleft lip and palate repairs. I'm quite capable of handling those, or assisting with the operations, if there are already surgeons assigned to the cases."

The director's gaze was searching, and

there was a small silence before he slowly said, "If you're quite sure…"

"I am," she replied, making her tone decisive.

"Well, then, I will make the arrangements."

Rising, she gave him one last smile. "Thank you. Let me know went you have it sorted out."

After the usual courtesies, she left him, pleased with herself for having the idea.

This trip would, if nothing else, take her away from Francisco Carvalho. At least for a little while.

Just a couple more days until the Dos Santos operation, and the meeting room was filled with tension.

Or, Francisco thought, was it just the tension in himself he was projecting onto the rest of the team?

All, of course, except Krysta, who was exhibiting her usual cool demeanor, fielding questions and soothing nerves while going through the plan one more time.

"The doctors in London have assured us that the infection Mr. Dos Santos had developed has been dealt with," Jake Cooper was saying. "He's flying in tonight, and I'll be examining him in the morning to confirm their findings. The reconstruction should be able to proceed on the new schedule."

"Nothing has changed, for us," Krysta said. "I will begin with the nerve splice, while Dr. Carvalho prepares the fibula flap for implantation."

There was nothing in the plan Francisco hadn't done before, except in the past he'd had to judge the shape of the bone needed, oftentimes with less than stellar results. Now he would be provided with a template, allowing him to shape the bone properly and achieve the proper fit and height.

He'd also been used to bending the plate that would hold the bone in place on-site, shaping and reshaping until it was correct. According to Krysta, with the 3-D printing, using the patient's undamaged mandible as a guide, and the precision mapping of the injury site, that was no longer a concern.

The plates should fit to exact specifications, and the kit supplied by the company who'd produced them even included the screws needed to fit it. No more hunting for the right screws midoperation.

Yet, the nagging strain twisting his stomach wouldn't abate. Thankfully, he was a master at concealing his emotions. No one liked going into an operating theater with a surgeon who looked as though he were on tenterhooks.

Was it the operation he was worried about, or having to do it with Krysta Simpson, a woman he was fast becoming almost obsessed with?

Suddenly his life, which had appeared so orderly and boring, had become a mass of questions and unwanted sensations. It had been years since his equilibrium had been shaken this badly. And all because of a woman who seemed completely, utterly unaware of him in any way other than as a colleague.

A woman he couldn't stop himself from wanting to know everything about. Intimately. Just watching how she used her hands to emphasize a point, the long, nimble fingers waving through the air, filled him with the kind of blinding desire he had no business feeling.

Just then, as Jake Cooper added something to the conversation, Krysta's gaze met Francisco's, and tingles ran up and down his spine at her dark, intent stare. Her lush lips parted slightly, as though to speak, and then she blinked, and turned away toward one of the surgical nurses who'd asked a question.

A question Francisco missed, completely.

Ridiculous. Get a hold on yourself.

He would be less than useless to the patient if he didn't get his mind back on the job at hand. These feelings, cravings, could be dealt with later.

Dragging his concentration back to the meeting, he made it a point to avoid looking at the alluring doctor for the rest of the time, and took off as soon as everything wrapped up.

Although off shift, going straight home didn't appeal. Whereas up until now he'd been perfectly content with going from work to apartment and back again with few deviations, tonight just thinking about his silent, empty apartment increased his restlessness. Instead, he turned into a restaurant near the hospital, and made his way to the bar.

When his drink arrived, he cupped it in his hand, although he didn't take a sip.

He'd never minded solitude before. Even when caught up in the crazy world of modeling, of being Mari's lover, with its constant whirl of parties and galas and openings, he'd had to sneak away periodically, just to be alone. Never did he feel lonely, at those times when he was by himself in a hotel room, far from home, or even hiding from the press, sequestered in his Rio apartment. Mind you, then he'd also been studying, more determined than ever to make it to, and then through, medical school.

Why, now, did being alone chafe so?

Not even the thought of seeing his family soon lifted his spirits.

A hand on his shoulder startled him from his ruminations.

"Mind some company?" Jake Cooper smiled, and tilted his head toward the bar stool next to Francisco.

Throwing off his dour mood, Francisco replied, "Please have a seat."

Doing as bid, Jake signaled the bartender and, when the smiling woman approached, ordered a Scotch. On receiving it, Jake took a sip, and sighed.

"I needed that," he said with a wry twist of his lips.

"I hope that's not an indication of how much you're enjoying being here," Francisco teased. "I'd hate to think Paulista's is anything but welcoming."

"Not at all," Jake replied. "Just having some personal issues."

Tell me about it.

Francisco didn't pry. Not being the type given to confidences, he rarely asked others to share theirs. He'd heard around the hospital that Jake had brought his nephew, who now lived with him, to Brazil. Perhaps that was where his problem lay.

"So, what do you think of Krysta Simpson?" Jake asked.

Of all the topics, this was the one Francisco least wanted broached. Yet, there was nothing for it but to reply, "She's brilliant, and nice as well. Not always the case in a surgeon of her caliber."

"Agreed," Jake said, although he sent Francisco a sideways glance as he spoke. "I was a little surprised at Enzo's determination to have her do his reconstruction, but he told me she was recommended to him by a friend at the Mayo Clinic. Once I looked into her record, I could understand why."

"She's a star," Francisco said. "It's the honor of my career to work with her. Under normal circumstances, we probably would never even have met."

"Ah, and here she is," Jake said, without commenting on Francisco's statement. "I invited her to have dinner with me."

He accompanied the words with a wave toward the door, and Francisco turned to see the topic of their conversation hesitating by the doorway.

She was having dinner with Jake Cooper? The confluence of desire and jealousy driving through his chest stole his breath, so much so that when he spoke, his voice was gravelly.

Rough.

"Well, I won't keep you from your meal," he said, unable to tear his gaze away from the woman walking toward them, even knowing he should turn away.

What was it about her that drew him this way?

"Nonsense," Jake said briskly, rising from his seat. "It's a working meal, so you should just join us."

Francisco rose, too, all too aware of her sparkling, somehow serious eyes trained on him as Krysta neared.

"Hi," she said, her gaze holding his effortlessly. "I didn't know you'd be joining us."

Did that mean she was sorry he was? Was she interested in Jake Cooper, not as a fellow physician, but personally?

"I just invited him," Jake said, drawing her attention and finally releasing Francisco from the hold those eyes had on him. "Since we're going to be discussing Enzo's surgery and postoperative care further."

Krysta smiled, and Francisco's heartbeat kicked up a notch. There was something so beautiful in watching those lips curve upward.

"Perfect," she said.

Stupid for that simple comment to make him feel ten feet tall.

As the hostess led them to a table near the windows, Jake and Krysta chatted easily, but Francisco stayed silent, still trying to marshal all his faculties for the discussion ahead.

Just as they sat down, Jake's cell phone rang, and he frowned.

"Excuse me," he said, rising abruptly. "I have to take this."

He left behind a thick silence, which both Francisco and Krysta tried to fill at the same time.

"Are you…"

"What is…"

They both stopped, exchanged a glance, and then Krysta chuckled.

"You go," she said, reaching for her water goblet.

"I was going to ask if you were sure you didn't mind my joining you and Jake for dinner."

She gave him a long look over the edge of her glass, then set it down.

"Not at all," she replied, just as Jake made his way back to the table.

"I'm very sorry," he said, sounding harried. "I'm needed at home, so I'm going to have to leave."

"Oh, nothing serious happening there, I hope?" Krysta didn't sound disappointed, just curious and concerned.

"No," Jake replied with a wry twist of his lips. "My nephew is giving the babysitter hell, and she doesn't know how to deal with him. I'll see you tomorrow, when we go to examine Enzo, and we can talk after if need be."

Then, with a final wave, he was gone, leaving Francisco and Krysta by themselves at the table.

CHAPTER FIVE

KRYSTA STARED ACROSS the table at Francisco, who seemed more interested in looking at the glass in front of him than at her, and wondered where it all had fallen apart.

She'd thought there was a real friendship building between them, but somehow it had devolved into this stiff, stark silence. She knew she was being contrary to let it matter. After all, hadn't she decided it was better to have distance between them, just so she wouldn't have to try to figure out how to manage her attraction?

Yet, she did mind. Finding someone she could relate to, feel truly comfortable with, was rare. Sure, she had colleagues she felt kinship with, but that was strictly on a professional basis. She'd felt there was more to be explored with Francisco, but now...

It was at times like this she felt her inexperience keenly. Someone more worldly, who hadn't spent all their life with their nose in a book, would probably know how to go forward, but unfortunately Krysta had to admit she was stuck.

Then her typical forthrightness reasserted itself.

"I think I must have inadvertently done something to upset you," she said quietly. "I wish you'd tell me what it was, so I can apologize."

His head came up, and she was snared, immediately, by his gaze. It was almost golden in the candlelight, and her breath caught in her throat, a rush of heat cascading down from the top of her head to envelop her.

"Not at all," he replied. "And if I have made you feel that way, it is I who should apologize."

Interesting. And now her curious researcher's brain was fired.

"Then what happened? I thought, when we first met, that we were becoming friends. Was I mistaken?"

He looked away, but not before she saw the shutters come down over his expression.

"No." It sounded as though the word was dragged from his throat.

"Then what happened?"

Almost absently, as though he weren't

thinking about what he was doing, he lifted his drink and took a sip. Then he put the glass down with a tad more energy than was necessary.

"It's just me," he said. "I have problems opening up to people, making friends."

If she hadn't seen him around the hospital, had just met him elsewhere and they'd talked like they had at the gala and over lunch, she wouldn't believe him. But she had seen the wall between him and other members of staff, and wondered at it. Just then the waiter came to take their orders, but neither of them had even looked at the menus. Krysta ordered some sort of chicken dish, too distracted to force her brain to interpret the description.

As soon as the waiter left, and she realized he wasn't going to add to his statement, she asked, "Is that because you used to be a model?"

Once more she remembered the insinuations made by Dr. Delgado on that first evening, and wondered if they had anything to do with his friendless state. Now she wished she hadn't been so noble in not trying to find some articles about his breakup to read. Somehow, she thought they could give her further insight into this most private of men.

Francisco was silent for so long she was

beginning to think he wouldn't respond, but eventually he said, "In a way."

She waited for him to expand on his reply, but he just stared down into his glass, seemingly lost in less than happy thoughts. So she took the initiative, and said, "Well, I don't make friends easily, either, so we have that in common."

He gave her a bland look. "Somehow I find that hard to believe. You seem to get along with everyone."

Krysta stared at him, honestly shocked. Then she realized he'd mistaken her work persona, where her confidence was at its highest, for her overall personality.

"That's just work," she said, wondering why she was being so honest with him when she still felt he wasn't being as frank with her. "I don't have friends. I've never fit in anywhere, or felt as though I could trust people not to make fun of me—my lack of fashion sense, the way I always put my work first. Socially, I'm a dud."

"You're not a dud, at anything." He sounded genuinely outraged by her suggesting such a thing, and his reaction made her smile.

"Oh, I know my faults. And if I didn't, my therapist would tell me. I'm afraid of anything that doesn't involve my job. I've never taken the time to make friends, learn new things that aren't work related or even take up a hobby." She shrugged, just as the waiter approached with their meal. "In those regards, I'm the equivalent of a twelve-year-old. Maybe even younger. I know what people say about how I dress, and they're right, but I don't really care. In that respect, you should probably be ashamed to be seen with me!"

Francisco didn't respond until after the waiter had put down their plates and fussed about a little, before leaving them alone again.

Leaning forward, he said, "I don't care about how you dress. You're a brilliant, beautiful woman, and anyone you take as a friend is blessed."

It was her turn to look down, overcome with emotion. What that emotion was, she didn't want to think through, only knew it filled her with warmth and pleasure.

And excitement.

He'd called her beautiful!

Her, who'd had to learn not to react when others made fun of her looks!

"Okay, then," she said when she'd got her voice under control and started shifting her mystery meal around on her plate. "Let's start our friendship over, shall we? If it'll help, think of yourself as my Reintroduction to Interpersonal Relationships 101."

"Sim..." he replied.

But she was sure the hesitation in his voice wasn't her imagination.

Francisco looked down at his plate, not really seeing it, and picked up his fork, although eating was the furthest thing from his mind.

There was a sensation of being pulled into a maelstrom, and it made his stomach roll. He hadn't been able to force himself to tell her about Mari, about being accused of using her to get ahead. Or about being leery of people saying he was doing the same thing with Krysta. Yet, facing that kind of talk didn't seem as imperative right now as it had been.

She thought it important enough to ask what had happened to make him withdraw. It showed she cared and wanted him as a friend, and that's exactly what he would be, despite the simmering attraction making it hard to even look at her for any length of time.

Making him hard, beneath the table.

"What made you go into medicine, anyway?" she was asking, pulling him out of his half-elated, half-agonized thoughts.

"My youngest brother was born with a facial defect, a cleft lip and palate. We were poor. Very, very poor. My parents worried about how they would get him the help he needed, and what would happen to him if they couldn't. Then they heard about a clinic where they could take him for free, and we met a doctor there who agreed to operate on João."

"How old were you?"

"Seven." He smiled slightly, remembering. "João was, not surprisingly, a cranky baby, and I was the only one who could soothe him, so my parents took me with them to see the doctor. I was fascinated by what he was saying, and helped him examine my brother. After the operation, when I saw what Dr. Jimenez was able to achieve, I knew that was what I wanted to do with my life."

Those dark, sparkling eyes were on him, and it felt as though she could see into his soul.

"There's a clinic coming up, in a place called Aparecida. Why aren't you going?"

That surprised him. "I am going. In fact, I am one of the main organizers this year. How did you hear about it?"

It was her turn to look down at her plate, and it made him wonder what she was trying to hide.

"I overheard a couple of the residents talking, and looked at the roster. I didn't see your name."

"My name wasn't included because it was a given I'd be there."

"Ah," she said, seemingly intent on putting an exact amount and ratio of food on her fork. It was one of those fussy little things she did that amused and enticed him. "I signed up for it, too."

"Oh? You know there probably won't be anything too exciting for you to do, don't you?"

The glance she gave him was scathing. "That's the same thing Director Andrade said to me when I asked if I could go. I didn't get into medicine just to do the flashy stuff, you know. If I can be of help, I'm definitely interested, even if I end up just being a scrub nurse."

Francisco snorted. "I don't think it'll come to that. We're more than happy to have you. Although surgeons come from all around this part of the country, there's always room for more. And it means we can expand the number of patients we see, which is always a good thing."

She nodded, and silence fell between them, but it wasn't fraught, or uncomfortable. Francisco liked that about her—that ability to put him at ease, even when he was supremely aware of her every movement and breath.

Eventually, she looked around and said, "I like this spot. It's cozy, and the food is great."

"Haven't you been here before?" He was a little surprised by that, since the restaurant was near the hospital, and on the route to the apartment building where all the visiting doctors were staying.

"No. I usually eat at home," she said, once more carefully filling her fork.

It made him think about what she'd said earlier, about being afraid, and he had to ask, "What have you seen since you've been here?"

Her reply didn't really surprise him.

"The hospital. My apartment." As though defensive, she quickly added, "The building where I'm staying has a nice pool. I've used that almost every evening."

"Nossa senhora!" He put his hand over his heart, to show how sorry he was. "I have been a poor host, and even poorer friend. We must remedy this, as soon as possible."

The look she gave him, although outwardly bland, sent a streak of fire down his spine.

"After the Dos Santos surgery," she said, and he had the whimsical thought that the operation marked some kind of milestone in her mind. "Then we can discuss it."

But the thought of spending more time with her, breaking her out of her solitary shell, had taken hold of him, and he couldn't stop his excitement and enthusiasm. There were so many things to show her, to watch her experience.

"After the clinic in Aparecida, I'm going to my parents' home to celebrate my birthday with them. You must come, too."

Once more she bent her head to look at her plate, hiding her expression from him.

"We'll see," was all she replied, and he knew, from her tone, not to push.

CHAPTER SIX

ENZO DOS SANTOS was declared fit for surgery, by both Jake Cooper and Krysta, so the schedule was adhered to.

Krysta hadn't allowed herself to think too much about her dinner with Francisco. Doing so would have disordered her usually focused mind. Yet, at night, when usually she soothed herself to sleep with computations and thoughts of work, his image insisted on inserting itself into her head.

For the first time ever, she was eager to get through a surgery. Not because of the help she was affording her patient, but because there was the sensation of life waiting to happen on the other side.

As she scrubbed in prior to the mandibular reconstruction, she kept her thoughts firmly on the surgical plan, doing her best to ignore Francisco, who was doing the same at the next sink. Thankfully, he wasn't a chatterbox, and they completed their preparations in silence, which was only broken by the sounds of running water and the subdued comments of others in the room.

It was a little unusual, in her experience, for the room to be so quiet, but this was, for Paulista's staff, an event of some importance. There was talk. If the surgery was as successful as everyone hoped, and the imaging and mapping models were found effective, the hospital might find it advantageous to use the techniques going forward. It was an opportunity to make Paulista's stand out even more.

Krysta was sure they'd find the new techniques superior to any they now used. The time saved using the preformed plates, guides and the template for modeling the fibula made for a far more efficient operation. And the final results were better than any she'd seen in the past.

Looking through into the theater, she made eye contact with the anesthesiologist, who nodded in return. The gallery above the operating room was full, but she didn't think about that, either.

Strange how if she were going to give a lecture she'd be a frazzled mess right now, but although a man's life and future lay in her hands, she was rock solid. Confident in her abilities.

"Okay, everyone," she said in Portuguese. "Let's get this done."

There was an answering murmur from the assembled team, and then they were in the theater, and beginning.

Surgery wasn't something to be rushed, but as they began, Krysta was highly aware of the time. The longer it took, the less efficient the new techniques would appear to be, and more stress would be put on the patient, who had already gone through one major operation.

"Retractors."

There. Now she could see exactly what she was working with, rather than just looking at scans, and something inside her relaxed, as it always did at this point in a surgery.

It was the feeling of the work truly beginning, although she was totally cognizant of how much it took to get to this point.

"The transplant site looks good," she said, aware that, because of the audience above, she needed to give some kind of running commentary. "Dr. Cooper did a great job of the mandibulectomy, and I don't see any signs of deterioration because of the infection."

They worked apace, each step as laid out in the surgical plan following as it should. Time ticked away, and Krysta kept a sharp eye on the other teams, but didn't try to micromanage them. If there were a problem, they'd tell her.

"Although instant repair of a bisected inferior alveolar nerve is preferred, splicing is still effective if done within three months, and most patients regain some sensation in their chin and lower lip within ten months. Not too long ago, the inclusion of IAN repair in a surgery of this type was considered too time-intensive. Now, with superior facial mapping and virtual surgical planning, it's become viable."

She spoke more for the benefit of the students sitting in the gallery, but it also was a subtle way of letting the fibula team know where they were.

"Performing the osteotomy now, Dr. Simpson."

Right on time. She glanced over in time to see the surgical nurse handing Francisco the Gigli saw, and then looked back at what she was doing. His calm, confident tone fed her own surety in the success of the operation.

"Nurse, make sure you have the template ready."

"*Sim*, Doctor."

There was always a chance that something could go wrong, either with the patient or the process, but Krysta was confident. She was preparing for the insertion of the shaped bone, while the dental implants were being placed.

"Each guide and template we're using today was specifically fabricated for Mr. Dos Santos, sterilized and packaged by a firm in Belgium. Using the template to shape the fibula saves time and eliminates any guesswork from the process. It also allows for preplanning of the placement of the dental implants."

Yet, even with that self-assured pronouncement, Krysta still held her breath for an instant as she fit the bone in place, and heaved a silent sigh of relief when it was, indeed, perfect.

"Less than two millimeters' difference. Good work, Dr. Carvalho."

"Thank you, Dr. Simpson."

Vascular work now, to ensure proper blood flow to the bone and surrounding tissue, and then the fitting of the titanium plate used to secure the bones together. Another silent sigh of relief when it conformed perfectly to the shape of the jaw.

"As you all know, mandibular repair in the

past often left patients with malformities of the face, making social interaction difficult. Being able to fabricate a plate that restores the shape of the face as close to normal as possible changed that. But it was up to the surgeon, at the time of the operation, to get the shape and height correct. Now, with all the tools and techniques at our disposal, we can save time in the theater, thereby reducing the stress put on our patients."

She went on to explain, when she could, about the ease of having screws specifically calibrated to the patient's needs.

"No more searching through boxes of screws to find the appropriate lengths. This particular company even sends correctly sized screwdrivers."

One of the surgical nurses said something under her breath, and Krysta paused to look up.

"Exactly," she said, letting amusement color her tone. "A dream come true."

Soft-tissue work now. She couldn't allow herself to think about the fact that they were on the final lap. If you did, things could be missed, or you could get sloppy.

Check and recheck. Making sure everything was in place, and looked perfect.

"As per usual, the blood flow to the jaw

and skin will be monitored every hour for the next two days," she said as she began to close. "Dr. Morales, our maxillofacial specialist, has determined there is no need for temporary arch bars to wire the jaws shut, so I believe we're almost finished here. Mr. Dos Santos has a long recovery ahead of him, but I believe he'll be pleased with the results."

There, the final stitches were in place and, for a moment, she hesitated, running through the entire operation in her mind one more time.

"Good work, Dr. Simpson."

It was Francisco's voice that broke her from her reverie, and she shook her head, looking around at the entire team, even as the bustle of postoperation broke out. Then she looked up, and meeting his gaze—warmly brown now—made her heart stutter.

She turned away, not wanting him to see whatever was in her eyes.

"No. Good work, *team*. I'm proud to have worked with you all."

Muted applause greeted her words and, suddenly exhausted, coming down off the surgical high, she made her way to the door. The surgery may be over, but there was still a long evening and night ahead, to make sure she was available, in case of emergency.

"Five hours and ten minutes." Francisco's voice came from just behind her, made her pause. "I believe that's a record here for us at Paulista's. You were *magnífica*."

"Let's wait and see the results," she rebutted, even though warmth flooded out from her chest at the compliment. "Then we can pat ourselves on the back."

But Francisco just made a rude noise.

"No matter what you say," he replied sternly. *"Magnífica."*

And, in his estimation, she had been.

Krysta ran a tight operation, without fuss or even a hint of confusion, and allowed her fellow practitioners to do their jobs without her constantly looking over their shoulders. She also gave credit where it was due. He'd seen the others relax and do their very best for her—not for the hospital, or even for the praise. Just to please her.

Such character was rare, especially among the people inhabiting the rarefied circles she was known to inhabit.

As he pushed through the doors into the men's changing room, Francisco considered the doctors and surgeons he'd met in the years since he'd started practicing. Just like in any other profession, some were nice, others horrid. Some were snobs, and yet others so full of themselves it was almost painful to behold.

Krysta fell into a class all by herself.

It was almost impossible for him to believe her when she told him of how truncated her life really was. She was the type of woman who should, after a surgery like the one she just performed, be taken out dancing. Be wined and dined and then made long, sweet love to.

Well, not right after surgery, when she would be exhausted and set to spend the night at the hospital, so as to be on hand should anything go wrong. But as soon as things quieted down.

Just imagining holding her, swaying to sweet samba music, pushed the edge of tiredness he felt aside, replacing it with longing.

Pare seu tolo.

Yet, telling himself to stop imagining such things, calling himself a fool, didn't help.

He wanted her, and when his feelings had gone from interest to full-blown desire, he couldn't tell.

"Good work in there." Jake Cooper came over to where Francisco was rummaging in his locker for a clean scrub shirt. The one he'd been wearing was soaked with perspiration. "It went well, from what I saw."

"You were in the gallery?" Francisco pulled off his shirt, using it to wipe at his chest. Did he have time for a shower? Probably not. He still had to check on other patients before he could even think of going home.

"For a time," Jake replied. "I was...otherwise occupied for part of it. Krysta had invited me to be in the theater, but I had to decline. Enzo may be my patient, but reconstruction isn't my specialty, as you know."

Once more Francisco had a moment of white-hot jealousy, and then he shook his head. Being around Krysta was making him a little *louco*, apparently.

"I think you would have enjoyed seeing her work, up close," he said, making sure there was no trace of his self-described craziness in his voice. "She truly is a master at her craft."

"I did get to see you work on the fibula flap. From what I saw, you're not too shabby yourself."

Francisco snorted, the sound caught in the fabric of the fresh shirt as it went over his head. "With the template provided, I would be incompetent if I couldn't get it right."

Jake Cooper just laughed, and turned toward the door. "We both know there was a lot more to it than just cutting out a pattern. Anyway, I'll make a quick check on Enzo in the PACU, then I'm going home." He paused for a moment, then added, "Who knew being a parent could be as exhausting as any day in the hospital?"

And before Francisco could figure out how to reply to that, he pushed through the doors and was gone.

Francisco made his rounds, and everywhere he went it seemed that Krysta's name was on everyone's lips. When he stopped in at the postoperative ward to check on Enzo Dos Santos, it was to hear he had just missed her.

"I sent her to get a little rest," the nurse in charge told him while he was looking at the chart. "She was trying not to hover, but failing, badly."

Francisco nodded, pleased with the readings he was seeing. "Did Dr. Simpson go home?"

That made the nurse chuckle. "Oh, I doubt it. I expect to see her back here in another hour, when we are checking the blood flow again."

He should go home, he knew, but instead, his feet led him to the surgeon's lounge. Opening the door as quietly as he could, he slipped inside. And there, curled up on a couch, he found her.

His heart ached at the peaceful innocence of her relaxed body. Without the force of her personality mobilizing it, the crisp, forthright personality retreated into the background, leaving a softness of lips and face that transformed her into a different woman. One that aroused all his protective instincts.

She needed rest. He could see dark shadows under her eyes, as though she hadn't been sleeping as well as she should.

And had she eaten at all, since the operation? If she planned to stay here all night, as he was sure she was, sustenance was necessary.

As though hearing his thoughts, she sighed, and snuggled deeper into the cushion beneath her head. A part of him wanted to go and set his lips to the curve of her cheek, the indentation between neck and shoulder, and he fisted his fingers to stop from reaching for her. Instead, he forced himself to go in the other direction, slipping back out of the room.

Although he tried to be as quiet as possible coming in less than half an hour later with a tray, as soon as he opened the door, Krysta sat up.

"What time is it?"

"Not time to check on the patient yet," he said as he walked toward the couch. Seeing her look at her watch anyway, he tried to distract her by asking, "Do you always wake up like that?"

That brought her eyebrows up, and then together in a little scowl. "Like what?"

"Fully conscious, as though you could pick up a scalpel and dive right into an operation. It takes me five minutes to figure out which is the floor and which is the ceiling when I first awaken."

Her chuckle was slightly husky, as though sleep still lingered there, if nowhere else, and the sound was delicious.

"No," she replied, watching him put the laden tray down on the table in front of the couch. "I was just dozing. Usually it takes me a minute to get my bearings. What is all that?"

"I thought you might be hungry," he explained, feeling a little silly even as he did. "But I didn't know what you'd want, so I brought some soup, and a salad, and a sandwich. It was all I could get at this late hour without leaving the hospital."

"You're a lifesaver!" She was already reaching for the soup, and her enthusiasm, plus the smile lighting her face, made his heart sing. "I could kiss you."

Ever after, he wondered at how easily the next words slipped from his mouth, propelled by a sudden longing too strong for his control.

"I wish you would."

CHAPTER SEVEN

KRYSTA FROZE, and Francisco did as well. For a long moment neither moved, and then his gaze dropped, to her lips, she thought, and a look she didn't recognize lit his eyes from within. Whatever that expression was caused by, it lit a firestorm inside her belly, and her breath hitched in her throat.

Then, just as swiftly as it had passed over his face, it was gone, and he chuckled, although it sounded forced.

"Desculpa," he said, reverting to his native language and then pausing, before going back to English. "Excuse me. That was out of line, and I apologize."

There was the urge to ignore his comment, or laugh it off. After all, it would be silly to place too much store in an off-the-cuff remark, probably made without thought, in jest.

And yet, she dearly wanted him to mean it, and couldn't help wondering whether she would regret, forever, not finding out whether he did or not.

But the thought of asking him was terrifying. Not only would she be opening herself up to rejection from a man she deeply admired and wanted more than anything in the world, but also risking a friendship she cherished. She could see no benefit to pursuing it.

Unless he *hadn't* been joking…

Then she reminded herself, wasn't she supposed to be conquering her fears, trying new things? It wasn't as though, if he rejected her, she'd have to see him forever and ever. It would just be a matter of toughing it out for a couple of months, and putting the humiliation behind her and moving on.

Even with that staunch pep talk, her heart rate was through the roof and her hands started sweating as she looked at him and said, "Only apologize if you didn't mean it."

He'd adopted his stone face, the one he showed the world most of the time, but as her words sunk in, it fell away to be replaced with an expression she couldn't interpret. Was it pleasure? Hesitation?

A combination of the two?

With a low-voiced mutter that sounded suspiciously like a curse, he stepped forward to sink down onto the couch, as though his legs didn't want to hold him aloft anymore.

Krysta knew the feeling. She didn't think she could stand, she was trembling so hard. How she wished she had even a modicum of poise right now! But she was trying so hard to fake it until she made it, she once more reached for the soup, and then decided on the salad instead. At least if that fell into her lap she didn't risk getting burned.

"I withdraw my apology, then," he said, rather stiffly. "I most certainly do want to kiss you."

Her heart leaped. She'd never known what that meant, only read the expression in books and thought it silly, until now. It leaped and stuttered, and what little sangfroid she'd managed to gather together fled, to be replaced with wild anticipation.

Then she looked over and found him once more staring at her lips, his expression now one of uninhibited hunger. Instinctively, she leaned a little closer, saw him do the same, and everything inside her stilled, waiting.

Wanting.

Then he took a deep breath and, shaking his head just once, reached out to touch her cheek.

"I want to, but not here. Not now, while

you are tired and worried about our patient. Away from the hospital, where I can have your undivided attention."

Krysta wanted to argue, disappointment like a cold rock in her stomach. She hadn't given even half a thought to Enzo Dos Santos in the last minutes, much less anything else. But she bit her tongue, and busied herself trying to open the container now perched on her lap. Somehow his words steadied her, made her wonder if he were just trying to brush her off gently.

Or, perhaps, was thinking about his reputation at Paulista's.

Not that she blamed him, really, if that were the case. She'd given in to her curiosity and looked up the articles about his breakup online and realized why he was so cautious. He'd been excoriated in the press, accused of using the young woman in ways Krysta found hard to believe. She'd found herself glaring at a picture of his ex, somehow absolutely certain there was a great deal more to the story than had been reported, but no one seemed interested in asking Francisco for his side. Krysta wished she had the guts to ask for it herself, but didn't.

"Damn it," she muttered, still unable to get the salad open, and when a large, warm hand covered hers, it brought her to immediate motionlessness.

There was a tingle, like static electricity, running up her arm from where their skin touched, and she suddenly couldn't seem to catch her breath properly.

Turning her head, she looked at him again, was effortlessly caught and held by his tawny, hooded gaze.

"Querida." His voice was low and soft, a caress to her ears that she felt down to her toes. "Spend the day with me, after you feel comfortable with leaving Senhor Dos Santos to others' care. We will find something to do, just the two of us. Then, if you still desire it, we will kiss."

Why not now, or tomorrow?

But she knew why, and was secretly grateful. Tomorrow would be taken up with monitoring Enzo, and finalizing both her next lecture and the planned clinic excursion.

Thinking of the trip to Aparecida made her go hot, and then cold. They would be completely away from Paulista's, and perhaps could spend some time alone, far from prying eyes. Then she stopped her crazy imagination from running away with her good sense. They would be working, surrounded by people, and then, if she agreed to go with him to his parents' home, there would be his family to contend with.

"Fale comigo," he said. *Speak to me.* And she realized she'd been sitting there silently, staring at him like a ninny, while he had no idea what was going through her mind.

"Yes," she said, as though she hadn't had second, third, fourth thoughts. "We'll do that."

He sighed, and gently took the salad container from her hand.

"Good. *Obrigado.*"

"Don't thank me," she said with not a small amount of tartness in her voice. Equilibrium was returning, with a vengeance, and there was so much she needed to think through before that day out with him. "You have no idea what you're getting into."

That made him chuckle as he handed her the now-open salad, and reached to snag her a fork. "I will take my chances," was all he said, and then, much to her relief, changed the subject.

When another surgeon came in, rubbing his eyes and yawning, they were discussing Enzo's operation, and arguing over how much of the new technology could be used in other applications.

After one more check on their patient,

Francisco left to go home, as he was operating again early the following morning. Krysta booted up her laptop and tried to do some work, but her brain wouldn't stop going back to their conversation earlier.

That moment when she thought he might kiss her, and how much she wished it had happened.

Had she really opened the door to something more than friendship with him?

Yes, she had. And while it made her sort of proud, it also scared her silly.

It was at times like this she wished she wasn't so solitary and had someone she could confide in.

Unfortunately, she didn't and so had to deal with it herself.

As she made her way back to the PACU to do her hourly check, she wondered how long it would take for the nurses to try to get her to leave. There was, after all, a surgeon on duty in case of emergency, but they'd find it an impossible task to turf her out. She always stayed in the hospital after an important surgery, feeling a sense of responsibility perhaps out of proportion to the situation. While they had used some newer techniques, the operation itself, its risks and long-term effects, were the same, and nothing new to Paulista's staff.

Nearing Enzo Dos Santos's cubicle, she saw Roque Cardoza coming toward her along the corridor. He was leaning rather heavily on his cane, and his face looked a little drawn, as though he had had a long day, and was paying for it.

They met up at the entrance to the cubicle, and she was subjected to an intent look, before he held out his hand.

"We haven't met. I'm Roque Cardoza."

As Krysta shook his hand, she recalled the conversation with Amy and Flávia outside the elevator, and thought:

I think he's rather handsome, too, although not as handsome as Francisco.

But all she said was, "Orthopedics, isn't it? Nice to meet you, Dr. Cardoza."

That brought a lift of one eyebrow, and a twist of the edge of his lips, as though he were remembering when they'd last seen each other.

"I am a friend of Enzo's, so I thought I would check in on him, and see if Lizbet needs anything, but I see she's not here."

Krysta glanced into the cubicle, and replied, "I'm sure she'll be back momentarily.

Since she was allowed in, his wife has hardly left his side."

"They are devoted," he said in his deep, accented tones. "One to the other. This has been a trying time for her."

The affection in his voice was clear, and she couldn't help asking, "How do you know the Dos Santoses?"

"Enzo was the owner and manager of the *futebol* team I played on when I was young. It was he who encouraged me to study medicine, after my injury."

"If he hadn't been injured, he would have gone on to play internationally, is what Enzo always said."

At the sound of Lizbet Dos Santos's voice, they both turned. Krysta watched as Roque hugged the older woman, making soothing, nonsense sounds in her ear, which seemed to both please her and bring her close to tears.

"Good of you to come, Roque. I'm sure he would be happy to know you're here."

"I will stay for a while, Lizbet. Has he awakened yet, since the operation?"

"Yes, he goes in and out for a few minutes at a time."

"Which is exactly normal, and how we want it right now," Krysta interjected.

"She is correct, *querida*," Roque said to

the other woman. "His pain should be carefully managed."

Then he insisted on taking Lizbet Dos Santos to get a soda in the cafeteria, leaving Krysta and the nurses to do their checks without her looking on.

It was only later, once more ensconced in the surgeon's lounge, while trying to catch a nap, that Krysta remembered how Roque had called the other woman *querida*.

And she couldn't help wondering if, when Francisco used it, it was simply as a form of friendly affection, rather than anything more.

The thought was so depressing she found herself grinding her teeth, had to force herself to stop. And when she fell into a doze, it was to dream about swimming in an unending pool, which offered her nowhere to turn back.

Or to get out.

CHAPTER EIGHT

FRANCISCO KNEW, because of his past career, people viewed him as a playboy, irrespective of the reality of his now rather boring, work-focused life. Yes, there had been some wild times when he was young and traveling with other, far more pleasure-driven people, but at heart he had still remained the same. A man who liked and respected women, almost a traditionalist in the way he felt they should be treated by the men who claimed to love them.

Another thing other people didn't seem to understand about him was the depth of caution life had taught him. At so many junctures he'd leaped without looking, and the results were invariably poor. Even at as young an age as six, the world had tried to teach him to be careful, to think before he acted. Then it was in the form of the spider lurking behind some scraps of wood and metal. His father had told him, repeatedly, to be careful there, but he hadn't bothered to listen. His reward for ignoring Papa's words was a spider bite that brought with it a great deal of pain.

All these things, he knew, had contributed to his not kissing Krysta the night before, when he'd had the chance, but he'd spent all his waking moments since regretting his decision.

Suppose his hesitation caused her to change her mind?

Yet he knew, without a doubt, there was something brewing between them. Something rare and lovely he wanted, oh so desperately, to explore.

This was all new territory to him, but he was determined to make the most of the situation, whatever it turned out to be.

"Are you all right?" Flávia's curt question brought him out of his stupor, and he zoned back in to find her eyeing him curiously. "You look a million miles away."

"Yes," he replied, bringing himself back to their conversation. "When do you think you'll be able to show us around the sanctuary, then?"

She gave a casual shrug, and continued packing her kit. "I'm not entirely sure at the moment. It depends on a few things," she replied, once more sending him a curious glance. "I could arrange for someone else to give you the tour, if you like."

"No," he said. "I think you should do it. Krysta knows and admires you, and she's particularly interested in your research. It can wait."

Flávia smiled, and was still smiling slightly when he left to return to the hospital.

He didn't know when the idea had come to him, but he was glad it had. Krysta had said she didn't make friends easily, yet he'd seen how confident and relaxed she was around others. Perhaps all she needed was to spend more time with people who, like Flávia, seemed particularly to like being around her? Sometimes, when you are used to things being a certain way, it took time and effort to realize they didn't have to remain the same.

He could totally understand where Krysta had learned to rely only on herself, and her own company. She had only been fourteen when she went to college! When Francisco remembered what he'd been like at that age, he could hardly fathom what she must have experienced. The emotional difference between a fourteen-year-old, no matter how academically brilliant, and the average university student must have been night and day.

Even when he started modeling, he'd been chaperoned by Caro, and so had been somewhat protected. Krysta, although still living with her parents then, would have had to navigate the new world she'd been dropped into on her own.

That was no longer the case, though. She was a well-respected surgeon, a rising star and, most of all, a strong, confident woman. There was no need to hold on to the old phobias and habits. Of course, it was ultimately up to her to realize that, and break out of her shell, but Francisco had no issue with trying to help her along.

It was well-known that Flávia also had the reputation of being rather solitary. She and Krysta may yet turn out to be kindred spirits.

When he'd approached Flávia, he'd seen the wariness in her eyes, and wondered if he was the cause. He was well aware of some of the things said about him at the hospital, and knew his past was the topic of both conversation and speculation. Fighting to put it all behind him, telling himself it didn't matter, and that only his work was important, hadn't taken away the sting.

The shame.

By the end of the conversation with Flávia, he'd realized her reaction probably had nothing to do with him, that he was probably projecting his own neuroses onto her. It had given him pause, made him consider what the situation with Mari had done to his life, despite it being so far in the past.

Yes, there would always be people, like Delgado, who would, without knowing the real story, be prejudiced against him, but he could no longer use that as an excuse to isolate himself. The people who knew him best, his family and oldest friends, knew the stories put out about him were lies, but if he hoped to make new friends, he would have to trust again.

The initial idea to arrange a visit to the sanctuary had started out as a way for Krysta to face one of her fears, but now Francisco wondered if it weren't as important for him to face his, too.

To face them, and get past them.

Making his way into the hospital, he checked his watch. Usually about now Krysta would message him, asking if they were meeting for lunch, but his stomach dropped when the screen was blank.

Had he scared her away last night?

Then his phone vibrated, and he unlocked the screen.

Just checking on Enzo Dos Santos, then I'm
free for lunch, if you are.

I was just on my way to look in on him myself.
Meet you there.

Not entirely true. He'd planned to make
a visit to the patient after lunch, but the opportunity to see her sooner was too good to
pass up.

In the ICU, where the patient had been
transferred, he saw Roque Cardoza coming
out of Senhor Dos Santos's cubicle. It wasn't
surprising he would be visiting the patient,
since everyone knew Roque had once played
on the famous team.

"Oi," Roque said in greeting as they drew
abreast of each other. "Enzo seems to be
doing very well. Even Dr. Simpson seems
happy with his progress so far."

"That is good news indeed," he said. Especially since Enzo Dos Santos's speedy recovery would mean Francisco could get Krysta
to himself sooner.

"Funny to see Enzo unable to speak,"
Roque commented with a wry smile. "But
he's already scribbling away on the tablet
they gave him, and once he's talking again,

the nurses may wish to have the trach reinserted."

Feeling more relaxed than he could remember being in a while, Francisco chuckled, then said, "I should go and take a look for myself, while he's already being examined."

Roque glanced at his watch. "Care to lunch with me? Or have you already eaten?"

"Sorry, I have a previous engagement. Perhaps another time?"

"Of course. *Tchau*."

Echoing Roque's farewell, Francisco hurried into the cubicle. Krysta was just finishing her examination, handing the nurse the handheld radar machine she'd used to check the vascular flow in the surgical site.

"It looks very good," she said to Enzo Dos Santos, with a look over at his wife, too. "There is less drainage than might be expected, and the swelling is already decreasing nicely. Take a look, Dr. Carvalho."

Francisco performed his own examination, after looking at the chart and readings, and he had to admit the patient was progressing well.

As they made their way to the elevators, Krysta sighed happily. "His recovery so far is going really well. If he continues at this rate, we might be able to remove the trach and nasogastric tube sooner than I thought."

"It helps that he was in good health otherwise, prior to discovering the cancer."

"Very true," she agreed as the car arrived with its customary soft chime. As they stepped in together, and Francisco pressed the ground-floor button, she continued. "And his attitude toward the surgery and expectations of recovery is important, too. I've told his wife to watch for any changes in mood or personality, explaining sometimes major surgeries can cause depression, or anger, and she's promised she will."

They were alone, facing each other across the elevator car, and suddenly Enzo Dos Santos's operation and recovery were the farthest things from his mind.

Her eyes were shining, and her lush lips were curved in a delicious smile. The urge to take the two steps necessary to press her against the wall and taste her mouth was almost irresistible.

The smile faded, and her cheeks darkened, until they glowed.

"Francisco." It was just a whisper. "Don't look at me like that."

"Or what?" he asked just as they got to their floor, and the conversation was abandoned, although, on his part, anyway, not forgotten.

* * *

Her legs were wobbly. It took every ounce of concentration to make them perform to respectable standards and carry her toward the cafeteria when they apparently wanted to fail her completely, leaving her a puddle on the floor at Francisco's feet.

For a moment, he'd looked as though he wanted to devour her on the spot—his eyes heavy lidded and gleaming, his usually stern mouth suddenly, thrillingly sensual.

How was she going to get through the next few days until they could be alone?

Did she really have to wait?

It was a question she asked herself repeatedly as lunch progressed, and the conversation between them slowed, then faltered to a stop.

Once more she wished she was more experienced, able to interpret what was happening, and how things were progressing—or not—between them. She'd come to the realization that no amount of intelligence helped when it came to emotions.

Especially for someone like her, without any empirical evidence regarding relationships, casual or serious.

Thank goodness this situation with Francisco would never progress to the latter. She'd never be able to sort out all the feelings, or be brave enough to try taking it even one step further, if she thought it would have long-term ramifications.

When he spoke, she was so deep in thought she started with surprise.

"I thought we could go to Ibirapuera Park this evening, if you are free. There is sometimes live music, and it truly is beautiful at night. And…" He hesitated for a moment, making Krysta's stomach dip and roll, since she didn't know whether what he planned to say was good or bad. "And I have a day off, the day following your next lecture. If it suits you, perhaps we could visit the beach, near Santos?"

She shouldn't feel such an intense rush of joy at the thought of going out with him, but excitement, and relief, made her almost light-headed.

"That sounds nice." Even to her, that response sounded lukewarm, but when she glanced up at him, he was smiling just slightly, that sultry twinkle in his eyes, and she couldn't resist grinning back.

And somehow, once that was settled, they could go back to their usual selves, comfortable together, or as comfortable as she could be with little *zings* of eagerness and desire firing through her veins.

After they'd eaten, and he'd told her he would come and collect her at her apartment at six that evening, he went to do rounds, while she hurried back to the ICU to once more check on Enzo. Knowing he'd suffered an infection after his mandibulectomy, she was paying special attention to his temperature and drains, but so far everything looked perfect. Her anxiety about making sure there were no postsurgical complications was beginning to wane, and she knew the surgeons at Paulista's were competent to handle anything that may arise. Therefore, she felt comfortable telling the nurses she wouldn't be at the hospital during the evening, and hid her amusement when they seemed discreetly relieved. But, of course, she left strict instructions for her to be called, should an emergency arise.

Forcing herself to go up to the small office she'd been assigned and go over her notes for her next lecture felt like punishment, but she did it, anyway. Of course, thoughts of the night ahead kept trying to intrude and, at about three-thirty, she threw in the towel.

She debated whether to go back to the ICU, but decided against it. There was a fine line between being thorough and hovering so much the patient began to wonder if there wasn't something wrong. Everything she'd witnessed at the hospital told her Senhor Dos Santos was in good hands.

Walking through the staff entrance, she found herself holding the door open for Amy Woodell, who was coming in.

"We meet again," she said. "How're you?"

"Good," Amy said. "Hanging in there for all I'm worth."

Krysta chuckled. "Me too. By the skin of my teeth, although with proper brushing I shouldn't have any such thing."

Amy laughed with her, then asked, "You're heading home?"

"Yes, it's been a long couple of days. I need a break."

It wasn't something she could ever remember saying before. Maybe Brazil was changing her even more than she could imagine.

"Ah. The Dos Santos operation." Amy leaned on the wall, as though settling in for a chat. "The whole hospital has been talking about it. Sounds as though it was a success."

"Shh, don't jinx it. But so far, so good."

"We should get together one evening. Have dinner, or go to the Morumbi shopping center. I hear it's fabulous."

"I'd like that," Krysta said, and found that she meant it. There was a part of her ridiculously touched that the other woman actually wanted to spend time with her. "Call me, and we'll set it up."

They spent a few more minutes catching up, with Krysta telling her about the Aparecida trip, and them deciding to wait until Krysta was back from that before embarking on their planned outing.

When they parted company, Krysta made her way outside, and started walking back to the apartment, but there was a thought niggling at the back of her mind, and she found herself stopping on the sidewalk.

What was she going to wear that evening? Despite assuring Dr. Hellman she would try to get out and about when in São Paulo, she hadn't really taken the promise seriously enough to bring anything even remotely nice.

Not that she really knew, or had even cared before, what would be considered "nice" on her. But tonight she was going out not just with a handsome, intriguing man, but also a man who used to be a model. One who no doubt knew a heck of a lot more about clothing and fashion than she did.

She didn't want to look too frumpy in comparison.

There was a part of her that wanted to scoff at the notion that she could ever be fashionable. Another part was almost petrified by the thought of displaying her body in any way. For so long she'd hidden behind baggy, unattractive clothing, telling herself she didn't really care what she looked like, as long as she was achieving at the highest professional level.

Now she had to admit that she *did* care, that she'd been using her ugly clothes as a shield against being hurt again, and she wanted to get past that painful night.

Perhaps she'd finally gotten to the point where she could, with just a little courage, overcome what had happened to her all those years ago, and begin to truly live again.

However, knowing how to go about it was beyond her talents. Time to find someone who would know better than she did. After all, if a patient needed a coronary angioplasty and a stent, she'd have no problem calling in a cardiologist.

A good doctor knew when to ask for assistance when the issues were outside their purview.

Before she could change her mind, she pulled out her phone and called for a cab.

CHAPTER NINE

THE LOOK ON Francisco's face when she went down to meet him in the apartment lobby made all the effort of shopping worthwhile.

The clerks had fussed over her, exclaiming at her figure, apparently wanting her to try on a mountain of clothing. She'd told them where she was going, and they'd eventually settled on a snug pair of jeans, far tighter than any she'd owned in years, and a beautiful silk top with colorful embroidery at the neck and sleeves. Then, since they said the night air might be a little cool, there was a jacket to go over the blouse.

The two women had argued over which color jacket she should get, one voting for black, the other for a fun orange, which Krysta would never, ever have considered before. Yet, when she put it on, it was instant love.

She'd drawn the line at the high wedged

booties they'd wanted her to get and, after some arguing, got a pair of low-heeled boots, reminiscent of hiking boots, but of lovely, soft tooled leather.

Now, as a slow smile dawned over Francisco's face, Krysta felt heat flood her face.

"You wouldn't look out of place at Fashion Week," he said. *"Linda..."*

There he went again, calling her beautiful.

If he weren't careful, she just might start believing him!

Taking her hand, he kissed the back lightly, and then spun her in a slow turn, so he could see the entire outfit.

"I went shopping," she said, her voice sounding strange to her ears. Breathless. Husky. As though she'd just woken up. "I didn't trust my own taste, so I let the ladies in the store help me."

"They did well," he said. "This jacket suits you *à perfeição.*"

She didn't tell him the jacket had been her choice in the end, but hugged the compliment to her heart.

The restaurant he took her to seemed a local hangout spot, but the subdued lighting and music low enough to be heard over gave it a subtle romantic tone.

Or perhaps it was the way Francisco kept

looking at her that brought romance to mind. For someone who'd never given it a second thought before, she found herself suddenly obsessed.

Yet, they kept the conversation light, speaking about places they'd both visited, and then the conversation turned to their families.

"Are you sure your parents won't mind my turning up with you for your birthday?"

"Not at all," he said. "My mother, in particular, loves having lots of people around. I think that's why she drummed it into us that it's good luck to celebrate your birthday where you were born. There's no such superstition—it's just an excuse to have us come home."

He said it with such fondness Krysta couldn't help chuckling.

"You told me about your brother João. Is he your only sibling?"

"No, there are five of us. My mother always wanted an even larger family but after my youngest sister was born, Mama hemorrhaged, and had to have a hysterectomy. I remember how sad she was then, for a very long time. So much so I sometimes thought we would never get her back, the way she was before. Eventually she healed, but I know how hard it was for her to watch all her children leave, as they grew up."

In his words she heard the explanation for why he returned home for his birthday, his tenderheartedness toward his mother another wonderful facet of his personality.

"She sounds lovely," she said. And then, to lighten the moment, added, "If she needs a child at home, she could take my youngest brother. He doesn't seem to want to leave at all."

That made him chuckle. "Why not?"

Krysta shook her head, as though in sorrow. "He's an artist, actually a really good one. But apparently he doesn't want to add 'struggling' to the job description. He keeps saying he's waiting to get on his feet before he moves out."

Francisco's eyebrows went up. "How do your parents feel about that?"

She snorted. "Well, I've told you a little about my father, so you can imagine that he's constantly grumbling about it, saying how, when he was that age, he was already out building a life for himself. He doesn't understand why Damon can't work a normal job and do his art on the side, like so many others do. My mom…well…she's a teacher, and always encouraged us to follow our dreams, so she hasn't said much about it. Don't get me wrong. They're both really proud of him, but I think they'd be happier if they felt he was doing better financially."

"Do you see them often?"

"Not as often as I should." There was no sense in lying about it. "I've allowed my life to become centered around work, pushing everything else, everyone else, to the side. It's not something I'm proud of, or planned on. It just happened."

"Well," he said in a deep, somehow serene tone. "It's never too late to embrace a new way of being."

Somehow, when she heard it like that, it made perfect sense, even as she acknowledged it would be harder than it sounded. She'd known, for a while, that her withdrawal from her family had hurt them, yet whenever she thought about going to see them, she allowed herself to be sidetracked by work.

And there was a certain level of guilt keeping her away, too. Not just because she'd distanced herself, but because she felt as though their lives had been turned upside down because of her.

Uncomfortable about admitting that to Francisco, but still wanting to talk about it, she said, "For the last few years, my dad has been saying how much he misses Saint Eustace, and longs to go back there to live. The only reason they left it to begin with was because of me."

Francisco tilted his head to the side, and said, "Why do you think so?"

"It's not what I think," she replied. "It's what I know. Mom went to the island on a teaching assignment, met my father and stayed, instead of going back to Connecticut. From all the stories they tell, they were really happy there, and then they had me. By the time I was two, Mom knew they probably wouldn't be able to give me the education and mental stimulation I needed. That was before easy internet access on the island. They made the decision to go to the States, so I could develop the way she knew I could."

He regarded her silently, his expression serious, eyes intent. Then he asked, "Do you think they regret how you turned out?"

She tried to smile, to keep the conversation light, even as an ache opened up in her chest.

"I don't know." She added a shrug, but knew she hadn't fooled him by the way his eyes narrowed slightly. "I'm not like other people. Not what most parents would expect or even want in a daughter. They never made me feel as though they weren't happy with me, but I never felt…as though I were enough, either."

He was quiet for a moment, then said, "If they cared only for their own pleasure, and had wanted you to conform, they would have stayed on Saint Eustace. But they saw something in you, something special, which needed nurturing, so they took you to a place where you could get what was necessary to thrive, and become what you are."

He paused for a second, as though thinking carefully before he continued. "I think you have come to live inside your head too much, *querida*. So used to trying to find answers to everything when, in truth, there are some things in life meant simply to be enjoyed, not picked over until nothing remains but dry and dusty facts.

"Take what you construe as your parents' sacrifice as a love gift, and be thankful for it. Family is important. There are so many who don't have one, or have ones that cause only anguish and suffering, so those of us who have good ones should be eternally grateful."

He was right. Of course he was. What her parents had done had been out of love, and she was eternally thankful to them. Making it an excuse to avoid them was both pathetic and juvenile and, there and then, she resolved to do better.

"Besides," Francisco said as he reached for his water glass. "If your parents were truly that homesick for Saint Eustace, they could have gone back long ago, despite your brother's determination never to fly the nest. After all, he could have gone with them, too."

That made her laugh, just a little. "That's true. I could see him as a beach bum, to be honest."

He laughed with her, then his face got serious again. "Most importantly, you are a wonderful, beautiful, talented and amazing woman. Any parent would be proud to call you their daughter."

Although she scrunched her nose at him, intimating disbelief at his words, she also looked down at her plate so he couldn't see the sheen of tears in her eyes.

He said all the right things. If only she could trust he meant them, but her insecurities ran too deep, and something stirred inside her, firing a determination to glean the truth. Just as she would if he were a difficult case, demanding facts to get to the basis of the problem.

She met his gaze across the table, and without hesitation said, "I don't have much experience in things like this, Francisco, so I have to ask, are you trying to seduce me?"

The shutters came down over his face, leaving only the stern, haughty look he so often wore around the hospital, and her heart sank.

But there was no anger in his voice when he replied, "Why do you ask? Is it because I call you beautiful, and say how remarkable I think you are?"

"Yes." This was too important to back down, even if backing down were her way, which it wasn't.

"When I speak of beauty, it is not in the way the fashion magazines mean it. I lived in the world they try to make others aspire to, and there is little beauty to be found there. For me, beauty is inside, shining out through the smile, the eyes.

"This evening, when I came to pick you up, it wasn't your new clothes, or even the fit of them, that made me say *linda*." He shook his head slowly, still holding her gaze. "It was you, who stood there obviously feeling good in those clothes. You shone, your natural confidence lighting you from within, only highlighted by the clothes, not caused by it."

He gave her a long look, then asked, "Do you find me handsome?"

"Yes," she said. "You're very good-looking."

That made his lips quirk into a wry smile. "And are you attracted to me?"

"You know I am." Heat gathered under her skin at saying it out loud.

"Because I am good-looking?"

"No," she said.

"Then why?"

"I'm not sure," she said honestly. "I've thought about that quite a lot, but haven't come to a definitive conclusion."

His smile widened, his eyes starting to twinkle. "*Exatamente.* It is the same with me. A fascination I can only feel grow stronger each time I see you. An appreciation of the person you are, and how I feel when I'm with you. It is many things, but not based solely on physical beauty, or physical attraction, although the latter is definitely powerful, too."

A shiver of awareness, of desire, ran down her spine, and her mind stuttered, shutting down for the moments she spent drowning in his dark, slumberous eyes.

Then she gathered herself together, wondering why he was able to so easily short-circuit her brain that way.

Did it matter, though? Couldn't she simply go wherever this led, without the constant overthinking? After all, this was her

Brazilian adventure, to be experienced fully, without fear.

"Maybe one of those things best just enjoyed, rather than dissected?" she suggested, and her body flushed from head to toe at his smile, which seemed laden with promise.

"De fato."

After they finished eating, they drove to Ibirapuera Park, and walked the short distance to the entrance. The grounds were a sight to behold, the trails and fountains lit with thousands of lights, which gleamed on the water, casting a dreamy glow over everything. When Francisco took her hand, Krysta moved a little closer to him, so their arms brushed as they walked. His fingers tightened on hers, his thumb caressing the back of her hand, sending tingles firing up from that point of contact.

"I will bring you back here, in the daylight," he said as they wove through the crowds. "It is the most gorgeous place in São Paulo."

"I believe you."

He pointed out the auditorium, which he explained had been designed by Oscar Niemeyer, and chuckled when she said the red marquee made it look as if the building was sticking out its tongue at passersby.

"He is my country's most famous architect, and this is how you categorize his work?"

She shrugged. "I have no eye for design or even beauty, Francisco, so my opinion means less than nothing, really."

He tugged on her hand, halting her, and his expression made her heart race.

"Perhaps that is another reason why I like being with you," he said, his thumb stroking the back of her hand again. "For many years I was seen only as a pretty face, no one interested in what lay behind it. With you I know, however my face may be classified and objectified by others, you don't do that. You see me, the man."

Then, before she could formulate a reply, he turned and started walking again, leading her on toward an outdoor pavilion, where a crowd was gathered.

The trio played a type of instrumental music she'd never heard before, but instinctively liked. It was called *choro*, Francisco explained, and was an older musical form that few performed much anymore. To Krysta, the guitar sounded as though it were singing, but in a language she couldn't speak, so she could only hear the words, not understand them.

It moved her, and she swayed in time to the enticing beat. When Francisco put his arms around her waist from behind, and they moved to the music together, the night took on a sweet, sultry aura.

Krysta let herself go with it, not thinking about it, just living in the moment, something she never did enough of.

As the final note played, and he let her go to join in the applause, there was a sensation of being lesser than she had been just moments before.

They followed the dispersing crowd along the road. Ibirapuera closed at midnight, Francisco had said, and it was getting on to twelve when they came to a metal bridge spanning part of the lake. They climbed to the top, and then paused on the landing to lean on the railing and look down into the water. As though the crowd was suddenly in cahoots with fate, the people who'd been there before them climbed down, and no one came to take their places.

It was as though they were suddenly the only ones in the park, and it was there just for them.

In the distance the lights of São Paulo gleamed, adding to the ambience. His arm went around her shoulders, pulled her close to his side, and she couldn't stop the little sigh of contentment that broke from between her lips.

She sensed him looking at her profile, and turned to speak, but the words died unspoken in her throat. The gleam in his eyes, that softening of his lips, sent her pulse skyrocketing.

Contentment fled, heat firing out from her core to swirl and whip through her body. Need flooded her as she stared at his mouth, so gorgeous in the low light. Stark shadows cast on his face would have made him look ferocious if it weren't for his eyes, the desirous set of his lips.

"This is one of my favorite spots," he said, his voice low and intent. "But tonight its beauty cannot hold my attention. May I kiss you now?"

Krysta didn't reply, simply lifted her face, angled her head and set her lips to his.

What she knew firsthand about kissing could dance on the head of a pin, but there was no fear or trepidation, just need. There was no one she trusted more to guide her, no one she'd ever desired the way she wanted Francisco.

It was a moment frozen in time, that first touch of his warm, firm lips on hers, and she shivered, the sensation so exquisite as to be almost surreal.

Then a deep, arousal-struck sound growled from his throat, and his arms banded around her waist to pull her in close. When his lips moved on hers, seeking, searching, her mouth instinctively softened, opened to the sweet sweep of his tongue.

For the first time in her life, her brain stopped whirring, thought ceased, and there was just Francisco and her and the glory of their kisses.

A sudden burst of laughter from a group of young people passing by had Francisco lifting his head, and slowly Krysta came back to herself.

Not entirely, though. There was, it seemed, a part of her that wanted to hang on to his neck and drag his lips back to hers, which was an urge contrary to the person she'd thought herself to be. Her cool control had been shattered by his taste and touch, the sensation of his warm, hard body against her.

"We should go, *querida*." His voice sounded rough, his smooth tones seemingly having deserted him. "The park will be closing soon, and we are expected at the hospital in the morning."

She didn't want to leave. If they could stay there, forever, his lips on hers, she thought she could be content.

But common sense won the day, and she let her arms slip from around his neck, wondering when they'd actually made their way there in the first place.

"Of course," she replied, surprised that her voice sounded so normal when her insides felt like melted wax. And it was only when he turned her back the way they'd come that she realized her legs were shaky.

The walk back to the car and drive to her apartment was a quiet one, both of them seemingly lost in their own thoughts. This was new territory for Krysta, and she couldn't help wondering if he'd found their kisses as thrilling as she had. If not, he would be too polite to say, and she wasn't sure if it would be appropriate to ask.

"I enjoyed the night," he said quietly as they stood in her lobby.

"I did, too." How tame that sounded, totally unbefitting the way little shock waves still fired through her system. Should she invite him up? Would he expect kisses to turn into something more? Was she ready to cross the next hurdle, whatever that may be?

Before she could find answers to any of those questions, Francisco pressed the button for the elevator. Then, putting his hands on her shoulders, he smiled gently. "Sleep well," he said before brushing her cheeks, one after the other, with his lips. "I'll see you tomorrow."

Then, as she stepped into the elevator, he left, and the bottom seemed to drop out of her world.

CHAPTER TEN

FRANCISCO BELIEVED IN patience, and in making good, well-considered choices, but on the morning after his dinner with Krysta, he awoke with a nagging sense of opportunity lost.

The taste of her mouth, the sensation of her pressed against his body, still lingered in his senses, and had him craving more, and more. The memory left him moody and frustrated.

Yet, in his heart he knew he needed to go slowly with Krysta Simpson. That, if he were not careful, she could turn out to be the heartache of a lifetime.

He'd also seen the hesitation in her eyes as they stood in the lobby of her apartment building, and felt she was worried about what might happen next. It had made it right to walk away, although no easier.

He knew if he'd stayed, gone to her apartment, he would want to kiss her again, perhaps go even further.

Not make love. He wasn't ready to take that step, might never be ready. Already his emotions were being engaged, his heart wanting to get in on a situation that was completely temporary. There could be no good ending for him if he allowed that to happen.

Krysta was too special, as a friend, as a colleague, to risk it all on physical satisfaction, no matter how much he wanted it.

He also sensed a deep vulnerability in her, no matter how well masked it was by her outward confidence. Perhaps the confidence stemmed from surety of her competence to do her job, but hadn't truly spilled over into her personal life. That would also explain why she'd immersed herself so fully in her job.

If nothing else, he could introduce her to a different kind of life. One where leisure played as important a role as work.

At the same time, it would allow him to ease out of the rut he'd fallen into as well. She truly had illustrated to him just how insular he'd become. It probably wouldn't have been long before he, like Krysta, had left a full life behind. But unlike her, he had no doubt he'd have turned into a lonely, bitter man, eaten up by regret.

He had her to thank for saving him from such a fate.

As he arrived at the hospital, he was called into surgery, and didn't have a chance to see Krysta, or even check on Senhor Dos Santos. He finished just prior to lunchtime, and made his way to the room their patient had been transferred to.

Enzo Dos Santos was sitting in a chair by the window, his leg elevated, a smile on his face at seeing Francisco.

"How are you feeling, *senhor*?" Francisco asked as he picked up the chart to scan it.

Dos Santos had a computer tablet in his hand, and scrawled with the stylus.

Ready to play football.

Francisco chuckled, and replied, "You may want to wait a couple more days before you get back on the field, sir."

The patient pouted, his eyes twinkling.

Still chuckling, Francisco checked Enzo's leg, and the outer area of the transplant, finding both to be healing well. The chart showed that the surgeon on duty had checked the reconstruction site not long before, and had made meticulous notes at what he found, so Francisco didn't check inside the patient's mouth again.

Enzo scribbled on his tablet, then held it out to Francisco.

Where's my pretty doctor? You're the second man I've had poking at me today. I prefer when she does it.

"I'm sure she'll be along soon to see you," Francisco said, but inside he felt a sinking sensation. It wasn't like Krysta not to check on her patient at least twice a day. In fact, he'd been hoping to run into her here, in Enzo's room, since this was one of the times she usually came by.

Had what happened last night made her stay away?

But that was ridiculous. He didn't see her allowing anything not of the utmost importance to interfere with her work.

After leaving Senhor Dos Santos's room, he found the charge nurse and asked, "Has Dr. Simpson not been in, at all, today?"

"She called earlier for an update on the patient's status, and said she wouldn't be by until later this afternoon."

Thanking her for the information, Francisco made his slow way to the elevator, wondering if he should call her, or not. Then he asked himself a simple question: If they had not kissed the night before, would he hesitate to contact her today because she wasn't in?

The answer to that, of course, was no, so he took out his phone and dialed her number. When it went to voice mail, he left a message, asking if she were going to be at the hospital for their customary lunch date.

Ten minutes later, she called back.

"Sorry I couldn't answer before," she said. "I was on a conference call. There's a problem in New York I have to deal with as quickly as possible. I won't be able to make lunch."

She sounded brisk, a little impatient, and he knew mentally she was still wrestling with whatever was going on, so he said, "I am sorry to hear that. Let me know when you are free, and we will meet then. Perhaps for dinner?"

"Sure," she replied, and then added, "I'm sorry to miss lunch with you. I look forward to it every day."

Before he could answer, there was a chime in the background, and Krysta said, "I have to go. There's a video call coming through."

And she hung up without waiting for him to say anything more.

How silly to feel gratified at her saying the time spent with him was one of the highlights of her day, but it was small consolation when he went to the cafeteria and ate his solitary meal.

Apparently, being with her was taking on a great importance in his life, and he wasn't at all sure what to do about it.

"And can you at least tell me why the funding was withdrawn?"

Krysta tried to keep her voice level, but it was difficult. She'd gotten very little sleep the night before, reliving Francisco's kisses, wrestling with the emotions and sensations they brought to life inside. The last thing she needed was to wake up to the news her next research project was being canceled.

"I'm not at liberty to say," the hospital administrator replied. "But you know research funds are limited, and sometimes one project leapfrogs in significance over another."

A nice way of saying someone else had commandeered her funding!

"Is there a possibility of sourcing funding elsewhere? As you know, in the past my research has sometimes been subsidized by private sector individuals."

"Well, if you wish to try to find alternate funding, that's your prerogative, although you'll also have to get it passed by the board of directors."

That would set her back months.

By the time she hung up, she was seething with frustration. They knew full well her past research had garnered the hospital both acclaim and financial benefit. Knowing they'd pulled her funding and given it to someone else was infuriating.

But it wasn't the first time something like this had happened. In her earlier days it had occurred with anxiety-inducing regularity. She'd thought she was past that point in her career, but apparently not.

Throwing herself back on the couch, she stared up at the ceiling, trying to decide what to do next. She loved being on rotation at the hospital, diagnosing otolaryngologic diseases and operating whenever something fell within her specialty, but research had always been even more important. It filled her life, keeping her engaged and at the forefront of new technology and methods.

Maybe she should fly back and petition the board in person? It felt as though they were taking advantage of her absence to mess around with the funding. With her contract coming up for renewal, was this someone's way of making her seem unimportant to the hospital? Expendable?

The thought infuriated her, and she'd actually sat up and pulled her computer closer, to look up flights, when she realized she was shaking, and her stomach was rolling. Despite the cool air of the room, a sheen of perspiration covered her face.

That brought her up short, and forced her to take a long, hard look at herself.

She'd made a commitment to Paulista's, to Enzo Dos Santos, and yet she was contemplating jumping on a plane, risking her reputation for reliability, just because her funding fell through? When had she allowed her love of work to become such a driving obsession?

And *why* had she allowed it?

Work was the altar on which she'd sacrificed everything—family, friendships, relationships—and now, looking out the window at the blue Brazilian sky, she felt hollow. Not at the thought of losing the grant, but at what her life, such as it was, had become.

Her work defined her, was the yardstick by which she measured herself. So much so that any disruption in it threw her into a tailspin.

Dr. Hellman had tried to get her to see it, in the weird, roundabout way psychologists had of getting their point across. When she'd expressed guilt at missing her parents' anniversary party, instead of focusing on the guilt, Dr. Hellman had made her explain why she'd missed it. When she'd admitted to not having hobbies, or good friends outside of work, the other woman had asked why. Almost every question regarding her lack of a normal, healthy social and interpersonal life had the same answer.

Work.

Research.

Staying relevant in her field.

Now she considered herself the poster child for dysfunction when it came to life.

Real life.

And she had to ask herself: Was this any way to live?

Even the resolve reached last night, when speaking to Francisco, about doing better by her parents had flown out of her head the moment work entered the picture.

What was the worst that could happen should her project get shelved?

The thought of it made her stomach roil. The physical reaction made her gasp, and blink against the tears suddenly prickling the backs of her eyes.

Her first instinct was to push the thought away as untenable. Then she forced her mind to hold it, sit with it, let it percolate.

As she did, her stomach settled, and calm descended.

What would happen?

She'd have free time, to see her parents, go wherever she wanted, although where that was, she had no idea just yet.

There would be time to do other things, learn something new, not because it was important for work, but just because.

Allow herself to be spontaneous occasionally, rather than letting her compulsion to plan every little thing order her days.

And all the prep work she'd been doing while in Brazil would no longer be necessary, and she could spend more time with Francisco.

Once more her stomach dipped, but it wasn't just fear causing her reaction this time. There was an element of excitement mixed in, and the memory of being in his arms, his lips on hers, pushed trepidation aside.

Settling back against the couch, she closed her eyes to heighten the recall of those moments.

His muscular body fitted against hers, firm mouth softened and sensual with passion, the satiny sensation of his hair between her fingers. It all rushed back, and a little moan of pleasure whispered from her throat.

It had been delicious. Sublime. And left her with an interminable ache she'd never truly experienced before but recognized for what it was.

Sexual need.

Another facet of life she'd never explored, out of fear, and now wanted to.

The thought of only being in Brazil for a short time shouldn't be an impediment to sleeping with Francisco, if he were willing. In fact, it would be the perfect opportunity. She wasn't interested in a long-term relationship, but she liked him, a lot, and found him more attractive than any man she'd met before. He, no doubt, would be glad to know she wouldn't be around for much longer, and therefore wouldn't be expecting a commitment of any kind.

Would he be willing, though? And how on earth would she find that out?

She wasn't so naive as to think a few kisses in a romantic setting meant he wanted to sleep with her, or that there mightn't be some other reason why he wouldn't want to.

Despite her just-made choice to be more spontaneous, this wasn't something she wanted left to chance. No, there needed to be a plan.

Could she somehow seduce him, like she thought he had been doing when he complimented her last night?

That seemed a nonstarter, since she hadn't the first clue how to go about something like that, and deemed the possible humiliation quotient too high if she got it wrong.

But how else did people signal their sexual interest in someone else? Should she research it, and try to glean more information?

She stopped herself. While she was a champion researcher in the medical field, thinking about hunting for the answers to this conundrum online felt wrong. Forced. Instead, wouldn't it be better to simply be herself, the new self she was discovering, and take it from there?

A glance at her watch told her Francisco would have had lunch already, and be on his rounds. While there was an urge to rush over to the hospital right away, she also had a lecture to give in the morning, and needed to make sure all her notes and slides were in order. One thing that helped her overcome her horrendous stage fright was meticulous planning, so she at least knew she was fully prepared. If she went to check on her patient now, she could spend the rest of the afternoon going over her presentation, one more time.

It would mean not seeing Francisco until dinnertime, but although she'd decided to turn over a new, less-strict leaf, today wasn't the day to wing it.

After all, even if Brazil changed her fundamentally, she still needed her reputation to keep her job, and that was, in the end, what was most important.

No matter what any other part of her anatomy tried to say!

CHAPTER ELEVEN

THE NEXT DAY seemed to pass at a rate best described as glacial, but she'd surprised herself with her reaction to having to once more speak in front of the crowd of doctors. While, when she awoke in the morning, she'd felt her usual queasiness, by the time she got to the hospital and entered the building, it had started to wane.

Seeing Francisco waiting for her didn't hurt, either.

"Ah, here you are," he said, that tiny smile playing around his lips, making her salivate for another taste of them. "How're you feeling?"

"Good," she replied as they walked together toward the lecture hall, and she sternly admonished herself to keep her mind on business. "How did your operation go last night?"

There had been a horrendous accident in the late afternoon, and the survivors had been brought to Paulista's. Francisco had been in theater when she arrived to check on Enzo, and had texted at five thirty to say he was unfortunately unable to make their dinner date.

She'd been disappointed, but took it in stride. After all, how many times had she been in theater only to find out that what she thought would be a two-hour operation stretched on to five?

"The facial trauma was severe. So much so that she lost her eye. The orbital structure was shattered, and I spent most of the operation trying to retrieve as many bone splinters as were safely possible."

They got to the door of the waiting area beside the auditorium, and he opened it for her, allowing her to precede him into the room as he continued. "Should she survive, which is still in question, she will need extensive reconstruction, including of the orbital floor. Since her other eye socket is undamaged, it would be a perfect case for your techniques, but unfortunately I doubt she would be able to afford it."

"Well, some of the companies are willing to do some pro bono work, or at a lesser cost, in the hopes of developing a relationship with a new hospital. Let me know, I'll approach the Belgian firm."

They'd discussed the injuries and future prospective operations and, before she'd known it, an assistant came to tell her it was time.

"Before you go," Francisco said quietly as she got up to head for the stage. "Are we still on for tomorrow?"

"Sure," she replied, trying not to let how much she was looking forward to it show.

And from that moment on, it felt as though the day ground almost to a halt. Never before had she been so impatient to finish giving a lecture, and less than completely focused. Getting through it felt sort of like a slog through mud, despite her love of the subject matter.

Then, before she could leave, the director cornered her, and invited her to lunch with him and the head of surgery. It wouldn't be politic to decline, so off they went to a restaurant a few miles from the hospital, and had the longest lunch she could ever remember. Both men were charming and articulate, so it wasn't boring, but she chafed at having to be there, rather than with Francisco.

Figuring it was as good a time as any, she floated the idea of approaching the 3-D printing firm about fabricating orbital floor mesh for the accident victim.

"Is it the same firm that worked on Senhor Dos Santos's case?"

"Yes," she replied to the director. "I've worked with them a number of times, and have found them reliable, cost-efficient and quick. It might suit Paulista's to have them as a contact, in case of need."

The two men exchanged glances, and then the chief of surgery said, "Let us see if the young woman survives, but even if she doesn't, I think it would be advantageous for us if you would put us in contact with the right person there. The director and I have been discussing the possibility of developing a program using the techniques and information you're imparting. It is just talk, so far, but if we decide to approach the board, it would be good to have additional information to give them."

She felt a little thrill of achievement. If they were talking about offering 3-D mapping and a more extensive virtual-surgery plan, her visit was already a success.

Getting back to the hospital, she went to check on Enzo Dos Santos, and found him not only in good spirits but also healing nicely. Once more, Roque Cardoza was keeping him company, since Lizbet Dos Santos had gone home for a couple of hours. With

Enzo's permission, she did her checks with Roque in the room, and thought, perhaps, her patient wanted a second opinion on how things were going. Luckily, she didn't think there was anything the other doctor could find fault with. Things were going exceedingly well.

"I won't be by to see you tomorrow, Senhor Dos Santos." Then she had to chuckle when he held up the tablet and he'd written *Enzo* in big bold letters. It had been an ongoing battle since the first day they'd met, but maybe it was time to let him win.

"Very well, Enzo. I'll see you in two days." He scribbled for a moment, then she read it.

Going on a date?

She wrinkled her nose at him, but at the same time a wave of heat washed through her, and it took everything in her to keep her face neutral and her tone unchanged as she replied, "Going to see some more of your beautiful country. A place that shares your name—Santos."

His eyes lit up, and he nodded, then wrote.

Beautiful beaches and gardens. Coffee museum.

Krysta chuckled. "I'll make sure to visit that museum. I'm a huge fan of coffee."

"If you have the time, and the inclination, there is also a lovely orchid garden there, too," Roque added. "And although the water may be too cool for swimming, if you surf you can rent a wet suit and board on the beach, close to São Vincente."

"I swim in the lakes up north, so I might risk the ocean," she said, without telling him the thought of trying to surf made her anxiety rise. Doubtful her athletic prowess would be sufficient for that!

There was no sign of Francisco, but a message came up on her phone, telling her he was going into theater again. The fates weren't being kind to them, but Krysta thought it was just as well. She still hadn't come to any kind of conclusion about what she wanted to do when it came to Francisco.

That evening, after taking a swim in the pool, which, for a change, did nothing to ease her stress levels, she impulsively picked up her phone and called her mother.

"Hello, darling," her mother said, answering after one ring. "Is everything all right?"

"Does something have to be wrong for me to check up on my parents?" she said, trying to sound amused, but in truth riding out a little wave of guilt. Her calls were few and far between, with little silences her mother always filled with chitchat, which always made Krysta feel worse.

"Of course not. How are you? How are you enjoying Brazil?"

"I'm great. Brazil is amazing. I think you and Daddy would love it."

"I've always wanted to go." Then her mother chuckled. "But getting your father to commit to a plane ride longer than it takes to get to Saint Eustace? Not an easy task!"

Krysta laughed with her. Her father's dislike of planes was a source of constant amusement to the rest of the family. A few times, while abroad working, Krysta had suggested her parents join her for a week, but it never happened, because her father always found an excuse as to why he couldn't go.

Now that she thought about it, maybe she'd inherited more from her father than her ears and the shape of her lower face.

"Well, if you were on Saint Eustace, it wouldn't be as long a trip. It's something to think about." How much smoother this conversation seemed, as if once Krysta allowed herself to relax into the give-and-take, it all became ridiculously easy.

There was a little silence, and then her

mother said, "If you were going to stay there in Brazil, we'd definitely make the trip, but otherwise I doubt it will ever happen. Your father is just too set in his ways. I mean, he keeps bawling about wanting to move back to Saint Eustace, but if I try to talk to him about making actual plans? He's suddenly too busy to think about it."

Oh, she'd definitely inherited some of her father's fear-induced deflection and avoidance!

Then her mother's words struck straight through her heart.

"Is…is that really why you've never moved back?"

"Of course," her mother said in her serene way. "Once you were old enough and we were convinced you could manage on your own, there was no excuse, other than your father." She laughed. "He's such a fuddy-duddy. But one day I'll pin him down and get him moving."

Krysta laughed with her, but there was a manic edge to her amusement, and relief made her light-headed.

It wasn't her fault that they hadn't gone back. She wasn't to blame. It was just her head, and maybe her ego, messing with her judgment.

Which other long-held beliefs was she holding on to that were, in fact, false?

Something more to think about.

And that night, when she finally fell asleep, it was to dream once more of that never-ending pool. But this time there was a current pulling her inexorably on, and a muted, distant roar that made her wonder if there were a waterfall at the end.

Francisco dragged himself out of the hospital after midnight, and drove home almost on autopilot. The last two days had been almost as bad as some he remembered from his years of residency, and at times the only thing keeping him going was the knowledge of the approaching day off.

And the time he'd get to spend with Krysta.

Yet he still hadn't been able to decide how to proceed with their relationship. There were too many variables to make it an easy choice.

As work colleagues, it could be deleterious to one or the other of them, or both, if they got intimately involved and then it fell apart badly. He'd learned that lesson a long time ago. When he'd started dating, he'd chosen young women in the fashion industry—models, makeup artists, stylists—because those were the people he was constantly around.

But on more than one occasion, with both casual and serious relationships, the ending had caused untold misery on jobs.

He'd wised up, and stopped doing it, hating the drama and the feeling of being judged a bad person because others said he was. Stupidly, he'd not stuck to his decision, and gotten involved with Mari, which had led to the ultimate in betrayal and character assassination.

He knew he was constantly under scrutiny at Paulista's, and didn't want anything to jeopardize the life he was building in São Paulo. There was often the feeling that there were some, like Delgado, who would be ecstatic to be given an excuse to get rid of him. It didn't matter the other man wasn't his direct supervisor. He and his family still had enough clout at the hospital to force the board to let him go.

Then there was the fact he wasn't into casual sex anymore, but on the other hand, neither was he looking for a serious relationship, having been so badly hurt before and being unwilling to risk it all again. It was a dichotomy that had kept him single and uninvolved, and sexually starved, far longer than perhaps was healthy.

When he was young, and ran with a wild

crowd, he thought nothing of sharing a night, or day, with a woman, and then moving on. There had been a couple more involved affairs, but only until he'd met Mari. He'd been crazy for her from the first moment they met, not realizing sexual attraction and insane emotional highs and lows didn't necessarily signify love.

After their breakup he'd become leery of entanglements, preferring to concentrate on his career, rather than open himself up to additional hurt. The women who'd expressed interest in dating him seemed more enamored with the thought of dating "Cisco" the ex-model than Francisco the man. None of that held any kind of appeal. Truly, no one had attracted him enough to make him change his solitary ways, until Krysta came along to make him wonder what, exactly, he wanted.

He had no answers, only knew he enjoyed spending time with her, and wanted to kiss her again, as the memory of those moments on the bridge replayed on a loop over and over in his brain.

Soft lips and body pressed to his. The sensation of sinking into their kisses, going down and down, until he drowned in her little sighs and sounds of pleasure. He hadn't wanted to stop. Indeed, he'd wanted more than was possible or feasible or even legal in such a public place. She'd aroused him almost beyond bearing, so that he had, for an instant, felt once more a callow youth, straining with desire, hungering for the fulfillment of sexual release.

Letting her go had been a task almost too difficult to achieve, leaving her in the lobby of the apartment building an exercise in willpower he still wasn't sure how he managed.

And tomorrow they would spend the entire day together, and he knew, without a doubt, he would be tempted to kiss her again.

He *would* kiss her again.

Which led him right back to the question of how far their relationship could go, should go.

It was a question that circled in his head until the moment his head hit the pillow, and exhaustion claimed him.

CHAPTER TWELVE

KRYSTA WAS UP and ready long before the agreed-on nine o'clock start of their day out, but at a quarter to, Francisco texted to say he was running a little late, but would be there in thirty minutes. It gave Krysta far too much time to stress over her appearance some more.

When she'd gone to the mall the day of their trip to Ibirapuera, she'd also bought a few more things, assisted, of course, by the salesladies. One of them was a new bathing suit, which was very different from her usual choice of traditional, all-encompassing, one-piece designs made to conceal rather than enhance her body.

They'd called it a trikini and, at first, she'd refused to even consider trying it on. Everything about it, from the brightly colored pattern to the cutouts on either side of the torso, had screamed "no." But the two ladies wouldn't stop until she agreed to at least put it on. If, when wearing it, she truly hated it, they would find her something else.

She didn't hate it, and had stared at her reflection for the longest time, wondering if it were really her staring back. The shape had emphasized her breasts in a way that should have made her uncomfortable, but instead merely reminded her she was a woman. The curved cutouts made her waist seem even more slender, and then made her hips flare.

Buying it, and the three sundresses the women swore were made just for her, had seemed a no-brainer at the time. Now, however, she was wondering if she were really ready to step out of her shapeless fashion box in this way. The sundress was fine, even if it did seem to cling to every curve when she moved, but the swimsuit she had on underneath filled her with disquiet.

Even reminding herself she was going with Francisco, a man she trusted explicitly, didn't help, and if he hadn't arrived a little earlier than he had said he would, she would have talked herself into running back and changing into her old stretched-out and unattractive one-piece.

Then he was there, smiling at her as the elevator opened on the ground floor, and her consternation fled.

It was the first time she'd seen him so casually dressed, in board shorts and a tight-fitting T-shirt that left nothing to the imagination. He was gorgeous, and she tried not to melt away to nothing just looking at him.

"Querida," he said, holding her shoulders and bending to kiss first one cheek and then the next. "I am sorry I am late. I overslept, which is not like me."

"Well, that's what happens when your operating schedule explodes the way yours has over the last few days," she replied, glad he'd kept his greeting so casual. Mentally berating herself for wanting to have grabbed him and given him a far more thorough set of kisses. "You must be exhausted. Do you really want to drive so far on your day off?"

"Hush," was his reply as they walked toward his car. "It is only a little more than an hour, and I want to show it to you. It will be far more relaxing than staying here."

Probably because he knew the chances of seeing anyone they knew while at Santos was remote. She didn't know whether to be annoyed or grateful he was being so careful about keeping their growing relationship private, although she couldn't help wondering why he did.

But she put the question aside, and they set out, Francisco handling the traffic with casual ease, until they had left the city behind. With it being a weekday, he explained, the traffic wouldn't be as bad as on the weekend.

"I thought we would take the older road, Rodovia Anchieta, on our way there, and the newer Rodovia dos Imigrantes on the way back. To me, Anchieta is more picturesque."

He went on to explain that the newer road was built to ease the congestion between São Paulo and the coast, since the traffic comprised both the movement of cargo and pleasure seekers. When the congestion was exceptionally heavy, the two highways would become unidirectional, with all vehicles going in one direction routed along one, and vehicles going the other way using the other.

A truck, going in the opposite direction, whizzed by at what Krysta thought an unsafe speed, making her gasp. Francisco's lips twitched in one of his little smiles, and he said, "I'm afraid you will have to trust me today. Sometimes the traffic can be a little frightening, but I am used to it."

"It's okay," she said. "In this I trust you."

That earned her a flicked sideways glance, but he didn't comment further.

The scenery fascinated her. Sometimes it was as though they were on an American highway, with carefully manicured grass on the wide verges; at others, the jungle seemed to press in on either side. Then there were the mountain cuts, which had her craning her head to see up along the slopes, where tenacious trees loomed above them. If occasionally she found herself wondering at the engineering it took to have built the road in the first place, she quieted the analytical part of her mind, and just enjoyed the scenery instead.

Arriving in Santos, Krysta was surprised to find herself in a place that reminded her of the fancier part of the Fort Lauderdale beachfront. When she said as much, Francisco nodded.

"It is a very popular resort for tourists and Paulista's as well," he said. "On the weekend, it's a bit of a madhouse, especially when there are cruise ships in port."

She could see why people flocked to the town. When she saw the beach, bordered where they were by a strip of garden, it looked amazing, with clear, light blue water and one of the widest expanses of sand she'd ever seen.

"We will go to the beach when it gets a little warmer," he said. "There are many places to see and explore here. I thought we'd start in the town and work our way down to the water later."

"Sure," she said as he parked and turned off the ignition. "Enzo said there was a coffee museum," she added hopefully.

Francisco chuckled. "Do you really want to visit the museum, or are you craving some coffee?"

"Both," she replied, making him chuckle again.

"Then both is what you shall get."

They stopped at a café, and had coffee and a pastry, and then continued on to the Museu do Café. As they approached, even Krysta had to be impressed with the remarkable building.

"Once this was the coffee-exchange building, and they built it to illustrate the importance of the crop. Would you like to take a guided tour, or just wander around?"

She opted to wander around, looking at the displays, recognizing the majesty of the building, with its intricate marble floors, stained-glass panel in the ceiling, and general opulence.

They ended up in the coffee shop, where

Krysta sampled some of the different blends available, and had another cup.

"You will not sleep for days, at this rate," Francisco teased, but he had one as well.

They visited the orchid gardens, which had a small zoo attached. The flowers and birds were beautiful, and she enjoyed watching the animals, too. The elevated walk through a tropical jungle got their appetites going, and after they finished nosing around, looking at the statues and arguing over which of the animals were cuter, they decided to go to lunch.

They found a restaurant with an outdoor seating area, and Francisco got her settled, then excused himself to go to the restroom. Krysta turned her face up to the sun, and realized she couldn't tell when last she'd been more relaxed. And happy. There was something about Francisco's company that allowed her habitual tension to dissipate. Most of the time she wasn't even aware she was stressed, muscles knotted, mind racing. It was only in the absence of those things she could appreciate how bad they usually were.

Lunch was a leisurely affair. The food was delicious, and she even had dessert because, as she told him, who could resist more coffee, this time in the form of ice cream?

"Do not call me at two in the morning

when you are still wide awake," was his stern admonishment, but the twinkle in his eyes belied his words.

Then they got in the car and drove toward São Vincente, where he took her to see the sculpture by Tomie Ohtake, commemorating the arrival of Japanese immigrants to Brazil. She thought it looked a bit like a dragon, but then became fascinated when a gust of wind made the statue produce a low, whistling sound.

"It makes different sounds, depending on the speed and direction of the wind," Francisco explained, making Krysta wish there was more of a breeze, so she could hear more of the tones.

They left the rocky shoreline where the statue was, and drove back to Santos, as Francisco insisted the beach was better there. There were few people on the sand, probably since the wind had picked up a little, but that didn't deter them. Francisco led her down through the gardens to the shore. Taking off her sandals, she sank her toes into the warm, soft grains, and sighed.

"Oh, I've missed the beach. I never realize how much until I get back to one," she said. "When I go to Saint Eustace, I practically live by the water the entire time."

"Do you miss it, the island?"

She thought about that for a moment as they walked toward the frothing waves, the sound of their ebb and flow like a lullaby to her.

"I didn't grow up there, so I don't have the deep connection my father has to it, but yes, I do. There is a part of me intrinsically linked to it." She hesitated, wondering if she should share something so deeply personal with him. Then decided she would. There was something about Francisco that called her to share confidences with him she wouldn't with anyone else. "There are times when I almost feel it calling to me, like a whisper on the wind, and I long for it so badly it's like an ache around my heart."

"We have a name for that feeling of homesickness, or longing. *Saudades*. I feel like that about Brazil whenever I am away from her for any length of time. Do you go back when that happens?"

Guilt tried to push its way to the forefront, but she wouldn't let it. The woman who ignored that kind of calling was slowly dying, leaving a new person to rise from the ashes. But she would always be honest about her past, too.

"Rarely," she replied. "I went more often

when I was young, and before my grandparents died, but as I got older, the time between visits grew longer and longer. I'm going to change that, though. It's a part of my life I shouldn't neglect any longer."

"That is good," he said. "You need to feed your soul, as well as body and mind. I'd forgotten that up until recently but, like you, I plan to do better."

Curious, she asked, "Was there nowhere else, in all the places you've traveled, that called to you?"

"Strangely enough, only Paris. I know there are many people who are not fond of it, but I loved it, very much. Perhaps because the French know how to balance those things that are important in life."

They had reached the water, and Krysta waded in up to her ankles, holding up the end of her dress. It was chilly, but nowhere as bad as the lakes she was used to back home.

"Surely, you don't plan to swim in there?" Francisco said, staying back from the waterline, amusement echoing in his voice. "It can't be more than twenty-two degrees."

Even though she was completely familiar with the Celsius system, she decided to tease him. Giving him a saucy look over her shoulder, she said, "Twenty-two? If it were that cold, it would be frozen. I'd say it's about seventy or so."

"You Americans and your Fahrenheit," he teased in return. "But however you want to express it, that water is cold."

"Not cold," she rebutted, reaching for the zipper at the side of her dress. "Here, hold my dress while I take a dip."

The flare of awareness in his eyes almost caused her fingers to fumble, almost made her change her mind and retreat to her old bastion of fear. But even more overwhelming was her need for him to see the new her, which, mostly because of him, was emerging.

So, before he could reply, she pulled the garment off over her head and then tossed it to him, the gesture far more symbolic than he could ever imagine.

He caught it, but as if by sheer instinct alone, for his gaze was fixed on her, and she saw his eyes slowly skim down her body, and then back up. When their eyes met, there was no mistaking the desire flaring in his, and her body responded, as if touched by a jolt of electricity.

For an instant, neither moved, caught and held in place by the knowledge of deep want, of arousal unleashed.

Then Francisco stepped forward, as though to walk into the sea to her, and the motion broke her free. Turning, she took a couple running steps into deeper water, then executed a shallow dive beneath an incoming wave.

The chill of the water did nothing to alleviate the heat sizzling through her blood. How could he do that to her with just one look? Swimming out a little ways, only the horizon ahead brought her dream back to mind, and she paused to float in the water, turning her face up into the sun in an attempt to quell her disquiet.

What was she going to do with these feelings?

Instead of giving her any insight, the ocean replied by sending a wave crashing over her head.

Treading water, she wiped her face, and started back to shore. Although she wouldn't admit it to Francisco, it really was too chilly for a prolonged swim.

Thankfully, he had brought a towel with him from the car for them to sit on, because the breeze, which had seemed merely cooling before, now nipped at her skin, raising goose bumps.

But he was there, waiting to enfold her in the soft terry, rubbing at her arms and back.

"You must be freezing," he said, deep concern in his voice. "Come up to the boardwalk and have a hot drink to warm you up."

"Coffee?" she asked, infusing as much hope into the words as she could through her chattering teeth.

That made him chuckle, even as he was leading her back along the sand, his arm around her shoulders.

After he had her ensconced at a table at an open-air restaurant with a lovely view of the ocean and heard she had a change of clothing in her bag, Francisco went back to the car to retrieve it. When he returned with not only her bag but also a dry towel, she thanked him, and went to the ladies' room. Luckily, because it was a seaside restaurant, there was a tiny shower stall, and she rinsed off the salt water before changing.

Coming back, she paused just outside the door to watch Francisco, who was unaware of her presence.

He was looking off into the distance, the set of his lips and angle of his head speaking of thoughts perhaps not entirely happy. His pensive expression tugged at her, made her wonder what he was thinking to look that way.

Then he turned his head toward the door and saw her, and the smile lighting his face made her knees tremble.

CHAPTER THIRTEEN

As he watched Krysta walk toward him, Francisco tried to push the thoughts nagging at him from his mind, but wasn't completely successful.

He'd had to acknowledge to himself, as he watched her run into the ocean, the intensity of desire she aroused in him, and it was a little frightening. When she'd pulled off her dress, revealing her body clad only in that trikini, it was as though he was a troll turned to stone by the sun. He'd been unable to move, to breathe, and then, like a tsunami, need swamped him, almost bringing him to his knees.

Instantly hard, desperate want shutting his brain down, he was about to go after her, take her in his arms—take her, there in the water—when she turned away, breaking the spell.

Thank goodness she had. He had been

about to make a spectacle of himself, and that feeling of being on the verge of losing control, completely, didn't sit well with him.

He'd tried that in the past, and it had been the worst experience of his life.

"That's better," she said, sliding into her seat and putting her beach bag down on the adjacent chair. "The water wasn't too bad, but once I got out and the wind got me..."

She shivered.

"Are you warm enough now?" he asked, scanning inside the busy restaurant to see if there was any space. "We could go inside."

"No, this is perfect," she said. "Or it will be, when they bring my cappuccino."

As though on cue, the waiter appeared with their drinks, and she put both hands around the cup, as though for warmth, before lifting it to her lips. Her little sound of appreciation made him, once more, have sexual thoughts, and she looked up and caught him staring.

"What?" she asked, but he could see how her cheeks darkened, and knew there was no need to reply.

As if in an attempt to dissipate the thick, sensual aura between them, she said, "How is your car crash victim doing? Did she survive?"

He didn't want to speak of work, but simply answered, "She is still in ICU, but the neurologist thinks there is hope she will make an almost complete recovery."

"I spoke to the director and chief of surgery about her, and they seemed willing to let me speak to the Belgians about supplying the orbital floor mesh. I'll follow up on it tomorrow."

"And I will apprise you of her condition, and when I think she will be strong enough for the reconstructive surgery."

Silence fell between them again, and it was the first time since they'd met that it was fraught, uncomfortable. She was looking down into her cappuccino as though the answers to all the mysteries of the world lay within it, but she was also worrying the corner of her lip with her teeth.

Francisco couldn't help thinking of how she'd said she had confidence in his driving, with the intimation that there were other areas where she might not be so willing to trust. There was so much he wanted to know about her, but wondered if she would answer his questions. One, in particular, he'd been mulling on since the night they'd gone to Ibirapuera, and felt compelled to ask. In the answer might lie another piece to the puzzle she presented.

"Krysta, may I ask you a very personal question?"

Her lashes lifted, and he was caught in the shadows of her gaze. The whimsical thought came to him that perhaps it was there, in her deep brown eyes, rather than the coffee cup, that the answers truly lay.

"Sure," she said. "I don't mind."

"Why is it, day to day, that you hide your body the way you do?" The shutters came down over her gaze, and the look of mild curiosity she'd worn melted away, leaving her expressionless.

Now there was the sensation of being on unsteady ground, but there was no way to turn back. So, he plowed ahead instead, wondering if everything would give out beneath his feet.

"You have said you're not interested in fashion, and I see nothing wrong with that. It is not something that is important to everyone. But even those who don't care about latest fashions usually try to at least buy clothing that fits. You seem to go out of your way to buy everything too big and, in my experience, that means there is a reason."

"In your experience?" she said, her voice cool and level, and just a touch sarcastic. "I wasn't aware you were a trained psychologist, too. Or are you a psychiatrist?"

He didn't take offense. "Neither, of course, but I used to work in the fashion business, and it is littered with enough neurosis and dysfunction to swamp the entire world. I know the signs."

Looking away, her shoulders stiff and high, she gave him her profile, as though ignoring his words. Her lips were tight, thinned by the pain he now knew she had squashed deep down inside.

Then she looked back at him, and he saw it all there in her gaze—an agony of spirit she probably rarely unleashed or examined.

"When I started college, my body was already quite mature, to the point where my mother used to joke that it was as if it was trying to keep up with the development of my mind. I never gave much thought to it. After all, at fourteen all I was interested in was my studies, nothing else, really."

She paused, looked down into her cup. Her long, nimble fingers moved over the porcelain, as though unable to remain still. Perhaps seeking purchase in a slippery, sliding world.

"I was still a normal teenager, though. I wore what everyone else wore. Tight jeans and tank tops. Short shorts or miniskirts when it was hot. I never gave my clothes more than a passing thought, although I didn't mind shopping with my mom and getting new stuff. And then, one night, when I was leaving the library, I was attacked. A man came out of the shadows, put his arm around my neck and tried to choke me, while dragging me toward some bushes."

Francisco froze, the ice flowing out from his gut inundating his entire being. And then it melted under the hellfire of fury. Keeping a neutral expression was the hardest thing he'd done in a long time. He wanted to rage, to demand to know what had happened, but reined all emotion in, to be what she needed.

Someone to listen.

Lifting her cup, she took a swallow, but now Francisco could see her hands were trembling.

Then, with a sharp clack, she set the cup down, straightened her back and lifted her chin to look right into his eyes. Now the fear was gone, replaced by something stronger, more resilient.

"I was lucky. My father was waiting to drive me home, and heard me scream. He'd also made sure to teach me some basic self-defense, so when I was grabbed from behind, I went limp, became dead weight, rather than starting to struggle. The attacker wasn't expecting that, and partially lost his grip. I got him right in the face with my bag, and then Daddy was there, and my assailant took off running."

A little smile tried to form, but died before it fully flowered.

"Daddy chased him, took him down and punched him hard enough to break his jaw. I was bruised, but alive, and I hadn't been raped, so I was very, very lucky. But I couldn't stop it from changing how I viewed my body. I didn't trust it not to get me into trouble, I guess, and started to hide it with baggy, ugly clothes. And even when I was old enough to know better, it had become a habit."

"I am sorry," he said, his voice a rasping mess because his throat was tight with anger and pain. "Sorry that you had to go through that, and sorry to have brought it all back. I should never have pried."

But she shook her head, and now a smile was not only achieved, but also reached her eyes.

"It actually felt good to talk about it, to air it out again and release it. He pled guilty, so thankfully there was no trial, but my parents didn't want to talk about it, and I had no one to confide in, so it festered. Coming to terms with it took a long time, but letting go of the effects has taken even longer."

Her smile widened, and Francisco's heart clenched at the beauty. It was a benediction, a bright, proud flame to chase the darkness of horror away.

"Here in Brazil, I've found parts of myself I didn't even think were missing," she said. "And I believe I have you to thank for that. So, thank you."

"No," he croaked, still unable to get his voice to come back to normal. "Thank you for sharing yourself with me. It is more than I deserve."

She shook her head, but said nothing more, and lightened the mood by asking what she should wear to his birthday party. Yet, even that innocuous question was laden with meaning for him, and he felt overfilled with emotion, proud of her bravery, touched by her confidence in him and moved by how desperately he wished he could have known her then, and kept her safe.

Daylight was waning as they made their way, hand in hand, to the car for the drive back to São Paulo. They'd fallen back into their easy ways, chatting and laughing, Krysta teasing him about his unwillingness to go swimming with her, Francisco snorting with disgust.

"I prefer my water warm, thank you very much."

"So, I suppose if, as Roque Cardoza suggested, I wanted to go surfing, you wouldn't be willing to teach me?"

"Not today," he stoutly averred. "Not even in a wet suit would I brave that water."

She just laughed, and called him a coward, and he readily agreed with her assessment, which spoiled some of her fun but didn't stop her needling.

By the time they were back in the city, it was dark, and he pulled into a well-known casual dining restaurant so they could have dinner.

"Ooh," she said, sending him a teasing glance. "More coffee."

"Are you sure you're not Brazilian? Your obsession with coffee rivals that of any of my countrymen."

After eating, he drove her home, and walked her in, as always. The lobby was empty, and as he reached out to push the button for the elevator, Krysta put her hand on his arm, stopping him.

"It's my turn to ask a question," she said, and something in her gaze caused his very soul to still. "Something very personal. More like a favor."

He tried to relax, to speak, but could only nod, and hold his breath, although why he did so wasn't clear to him.

"Would you take my virginity?"

Krysta saw a flash of desire in Francisco's eyes so intense she shivered, but then it was gone, and his habitual mask fell into place, leaving his expression carefully blank.

For her part, she felt no trepidation. He was the one man she'd ever met who she both trusted and wanted. The worst that could happen is he declined, and they continued on the way they were.

Or not.

It mattered greatly to her, but she was used to making decisions and sticking to them, and sometime during the day she'd realized she couldn't bear the desire without knowing whether or not it would be fulfilled. If he said no, then she'd at least have an answer, and could figure out how else to manage the changes she was going through.

He was still just looking at her, the arm beneath her hand tightening to rock hardness.

"Fale comigo," she said to him as he once had said to her, and she saw him swallow.

"You would ask me this, here? In the lobby?" His voice was as hard as his arm, but it wasn't frightening. In fact, it gave her another *zing* of awareness, edged her arousal a little higher. "Tell me, in one sentence, that you want me but are still a virgin?"

"Is that a bad thing?" she asked, not allowing her voice to display anything but mild curiosity, and a touch of amusement, even though, inside, her stomach twisted and her heartbeat was a ragged, unsteady thing.

"*Meu Deus.* Is this a joke to you? For it isn't to me. I cannot discuss this here with you now."

Releasing his arm, she reached back and pressed the button for the elevator, and then stepped in when the doors opened immediately.

Placing her hand to stop them from closing, she said, "We could discuss it upstairs, if you prefer more privacy."

He covered her hand with his. "You make me *louco*. I should walk away, but I do not want to."

"Then don't," she said, her insides melting in the way they so often did when she was around him.

"If I come upstairs, it will not be to take your virginity, but I cannot promise I will behave the perfect gentleman, either. Choose carefully, *amor*, before you tell me to stay, or go."

Should she be having second thoughts at his fierce pronouncement? If so, she'd missed some vital piece of information, because it did nothing but make her want him more.

She wrapped her fingers around his wrist, and gave it a tug. It wasn't enough to budge a man as strong as Francisco, but apparently all the impetus he needed to step into the car.

They didn't touch as the doors slid closed and she pressed the button for her floor, but their gazes locked, and the air in the elevator grew thick with anticipation.

Still silent, he stood back to let her pass when they got to her floor, and the doors opened once more. The ride had been only seconds long, but to Krysta it seemed to have taken forever. Beneath her skin her entire being vibrated with want. She still remembered how he'd felt in her arms, that hard, delicious body against her softer, more yielding one, and craved that again.

When she'd unlocked the door and stepped a few paces inside, she turned to watch him follow. He prowled in slowly, his gait reminding her of her initial reaction on meeting him, when she'd likened him to a wolf.

And when he circled her, making her have to turn to watch him, his gaze never straying from her face, the effect was heightened to a thrilling degree.

"You are still a virgin?"

He fired the question like a shot at her, and she started, her heart rate kicking up another notch.

"Yes."

"How? Why?"

At any other time, she would have laughed at the thought of explaining the "how," but nothing about this was amusing. Arousing, frustrating and a little frightening, yes. But not amusing.

"Lack of interest, would be the first guess. Not finding anyone I wanted, the way I want you, would be the second."

His eyes darkened, and his prowling, stalking revolution around her stopped.

"Fear? Because of what happened when you were young?"

She'd always been honest with him. No need to stop now.

"Yes."

"Are you afraid now?"

"A little, because this is all new to me. But somehow I trust you not to hurt me."

The fierce expression faded, and he scrubbed

a hand over his face. When it fell away, she saw a man conflicted—need and worry at war with each other.

"Eu te quero," he said.

I want you.

Then he continued, "But you must realize, sex changes everything. I am afraid that if we make love, nothing will be the same, and perhaps not for the better."

She lifted her chin, and said, "I'm willing to take that chance. Are you? And if you're not, I think you should leave now, before I come over there and climb all over you."

CHAPTER FOURTEEN

NOW SHE HELD her breath, waiting for his decision. When he finally moved, she thought it was to leave, and her heart stopped for an instant, but he only went as far as the door, locking it. Then he turned, and now her heart raced again.

"I know I should leave," he said, his voice so low it was just above a whisper. "And yet, the thought of not holding you again, not kissing you, never being able to know what it is like when we are intimately together, is untenable."

Once more he stalked her, closing in slowly, and her legs trembled from seeing the heat in his eyes. Then she was in his arms, and her brain stuttered and shut down as their lips met.

He kissed her with muted ferocity, and she returned it in kind. She'd spent too many nights longing for this moment, dreaming of it, and she couldn't get enough. The remembered taste of him fired into her blood, more potent than any liquor, and when he exhaled, she took the air into her body, held it for a moment.

His lips left hers to slide along her jaw, and then up to her ear.

"Amor. Eu te quero," he whispered. "I want to touch you, feel your skin on mine. I crave it, like water, or air."

"Yes," she gasped. "I want that, too. So very much."

Yet, he took his time, guiding her to the couch and pulling her onto his lap to kiss her some more. It was the sweetest of agonies as his hands skimmed her back and belly, the lower swells of her breasts through her clothes. Impatient, she tugged at his T-shirt, and he leaned forward to help her get it off.

The sensation of his flesh under her fingertips, the muscles rippling beneath, was fascinating and oh so arousing. Touching him became her focus, and he let her explore his torso and arms to her heart's content.

But when she circled his nipples, watching them contract to tiny peaks, he growled her name and pulled her hands away.

"Hey, I was enjoying that," she groused.

"I'll show you why I stopped you," came his rough reply.

He unzipped her dress, and she shivered as his fingers brushed her flesh. When he pushed the straps down, the garment fell to her waist, leaving her upper body clad only in her strapless bra, which he didn't hesitate to unclasp with a quick flick of his fingers.

Then his hands were on her, fingers drifting over her skin, raising trails of flames wherever they touched. She arched, wanting more, desire whipped to a wildfire in her body, immolating her from the inside out.

Just like she had, he circled her nipples, and she trembled, lost in the glorious torture. Then his lips closed over one, and she jerked, grabbing the back of his head to hang on, afraid she'd pass out, it felt so good.

He rolled her off his lap, lying her down on her back on the sofa, leaning over her to lick and suck from her throat to her belly. Krysta twisted beneath him, shocked at her body's response, the immensity of her need. Suddenly frightened, she pushed at his head, and he sat up. Whatever he saw on her face had him pulling her up into his arms.

"Shh…" he whispered, holding her, stroking her hair. "I forgot I need to be gentle, to take my time. Do you want me to stop?"

"No. I don't know." The breath was sawing in and out of her lungs, making it difficult to speak. "I'm overwhelmed right now, but I don't really want to stop. I don't know what I want."

"Krysta, have you ever had an orgasm?"

She snorted. "Are you asking if I masturbate? The answer is no. I told you, I locked everything to do with sex away, and refused to give it a thought."

He was silent for a moment, then he asked, "Will you let me give you one? I think, perhaps, that's what your body wants right now."

"Okay." She said it into his throat, suddenly shy, although she knew how ridiculous that was. After all, wasn't she the one who initiated this?

"Tell me to stop if you want to," he said, and then eased her back onto his lap. She leaned on his chest, her face tucked into the space between his shoulder and neck.

He didn't take off her dress, just slowly slid his hand up under the skirt, caressing her calves, then her knees, and thighs, moving up to the apex of her legs. It relaxed and aroused her, all at the same time.

How was that even possible?

Her legs fell open of their own accord, giving him access, and she found herself tilting her hips, longing for the touch that would take her over the edge.

When his finger slid under her panties and between her folds, gently exploring, she had to remind herself to breathe.

"Easy, *amor*," he whispered. "Let me take care of you."

His finger circled, awakening nerve endings, sending another wave of shudders through her body. Then the circle tightened, found its mark, and she stiffened, shaking and mewling and wanting to beg for culmination.

"There," she cried, her thighs tightening on his arm.

"Yes," he crooned. "Let it happen, *amor*. Come for me."

Somehow the words made it perfect, took her from frustration and need and threw her, body and soul, into swirling, beautiful, orgasmic satisfaction.

"Better?" he asked when she finally calmed.

"Yes," she said, feeling wonderfully lethargic. "But can we do that again?"

He chuckled, but it was strained, and she could feel the hardness of his erection beneath her bottom.

"Francisco?"

"Hmm?"

"If you won't make love to me tonight, maybe we should stop. I don't want to cause you more discomfort."

"Ah, *amor*, even if we stopped now, I would be hard for you all night. You are like fire in my blood."

She lifted her head to look at him, and immediately she felt another surge of desire chase away her lethargy. There was something about his heavy-lidded eyes and softened mouth that did things to her insides.

Krysta tried to move, but Francisco held her in place with his arm.

"Where are you going?"

"Nowhere," she said. "I just wanted to change position."

When he let her up, she slid off his lap to shimmy out of her dress. Feeling bold, she pulled off her panties, too, and stepped out of them. His face tightened, and her nipples beaded just from the way his gaze caressed her body.

Then she straddled him, her thighs on either side of his, and he groaned as his arms banded around her waist to pull her in tight. His lips found the pulse at the side of her throat, and she arched, loving the sensation of his mouth on her skin.

"*Nossa senhora.* I want you so much."

"Why not have me, then?"

"I don't know if it is the right thing to do, Krysta. I need to think it through, and I can't when I have you naked in my arms."

Leaning back, she lifted his chin, so as to see his expression when she asked, "If I weren't a virgin, would you still hesitate?"

"Yes," he replied without pause. "There is something between us, something I'm a little afraid of. You'll be gone in less than two months. I don't want to do something I, or we, will regret."

She nodded. "I know what you mean, but I looked at it from the other side. When I left, would it be with regrets for not taking this chance? Would I forever wonder what it would be like to kiss you, touch you, make love with you? And I knew the answer would be yes."

Taking a deep breath, she said what she thought they'd been skirting around the entire time.

"What we've found in each other is special, at least it is to me, but I don't want to fall in love with you. I don't want you to fall for me. Soon, our lives will once more diverge, me heading back to the States, you staying here. We have careers we're proud of, and want to keep building. Your family is here, mine is back home. It's a recipe for disaster, if we let it come to that.

"But this…" She gestured between them, touching his chest and then her own. "This I will never, ever regret, no matter what else happens."

His gaze bored into hers, as though he were trying to see into her soul. It amazed her how dark his eyes got, his pupils dilating until there was just a hint of lighter brown around them. And the knowledge it was passion for her that made them so gave her huge satisfaction.

"So, you feel we should make memories to carry with us, without worry or fear of the future? Slake this desire, and gorge ourselves with passion, because we already know it is all to end when you leave?"

"Yes." She nodded. "That's exactly what I think."

He was silent for a moment more, and then inhaled deeply.

"So be it," came his reply as he lifted to his feet, his hands on her bottom to hold her aloft. "Where is your bedroom?"

He knew Krysta spoke the truth, as she knew it, but Francisco suspected it was already too late for him.

That he was already more than halfway in love with her.

There was no future in it, as she had already so succinctly stated, but he couldn't resist her, didn't want to resist the passion that arose in him every time she was near. There might never be another chance like this, and he would grab hold of it with both hands, even if the end result was heartbreak.

So, he made love to her, taking pride in being the man who opened to her the world of passion, reveling in her responses, and the knowledge he gave her satisfaction.

Her body was beautiful, her lack of self-consciousness a turn-on unlike any he'd experienced before. She was a woman who, now that she had broken out from beyond the barrier of her inhibitions, embraced physical pleasure with the same enthusiasm as she did her work.

In a strange way, he felt as though it was his responsibility to introduce her fully to her body, and it made him more sensitive to her every reaction.

"Oh, Francisco." Her voice was hoarse, the words strained, as her hips tilted up toward his lips. "That's so good."

"You like that, *amor*?" He was teasing her,

wanting her ready for his body. "Will you come for me again?"

Her body tightened around his fingers, and her thighs trembled.

"I want you. I need you. *Please.*"

He didn't want to wait anymore; he wanted to be inside her with a kind of ferocious desperation he wasn't used to feeling.

Thank goodness he still had a condom in his wallet, although *Deus* alone knew how long it had been there. The last thing either of them would want or need was for her to get pregnant.

Yet, the thought of it brought him no fear, only a rush of longing so strong it stole his breath, and it took a moment for him to regain his composure.

Well, as much composure as one could muster when faced with the woman of your dreams, naked, begging for you to make her yours.

He'd done his best to prepare her but, as he positioned himself between her thighs, he watched for any sign of pain, or indication she'd suddenly changed her mind. Instead, what happened was, as soon as he started to slide into the gloriously wet heat of her body, she wrapped her legs around his waist and tried to pull him in, all at once.

"Gently." It rumbled from his throat like a groan. "Gently."

She only tilted her hips and tugged harder.

He lay over her, kissing her over and over, letting her get used to him, watching the play of emotion over her face. When he started to move in long, slow strokes, her eyes flew open and her lips parted on a gasp so redolent of pleasure it almost made him lose control.

Her hips flexed beneath his, adding a thrilling new sensation, and Francisco knew he wouldn't last long.

The feelings were too sublime, the emotions in him too strong.

Going up on his knees, he resumed his thrusts, but reached between them to find her clitoris and stroke it with his thumb.

Her eyelids fluttered, tried to close, but she kept them open, her gaze on his, as she whimpered a plea.

And when they found bliss together, Francisco knew, without a doubt, he was already in too deep.

CHAPTER FIFTEEN

KRYSTA WASN'T AT ALL sure what she'd gotten herself into, but whatever the outcome, she didn't want her affair with Francisco to end one moment sooner than it had to.

The memory of his kisses, touch and lovemaking intruded on her brain at the most inopportune moments, sending waves of heat through her body. Sometimes it felt as though she were constantly blushing. Keeping it all together, not betraying the change in their relationship at work, was exceedingly difficult, and she finally thought she knew what he'd meant when he'd said sex changes everything.

Keeping their interactions businesslike and professional at the hospital took reserves of strength she didn't even know she had.

It appeared, however, that she was doing a good job, as she discovered one day while in the ladies' room near the cafeteria.

"What a strange pair they make—Cisco and the American. Him so handsome and put together, her so strange and unfashionable. Do you think there's something going on between them?"

There was a giggle, and another voice answered, "She's not so bad. If she dressed better, I think she'd be more attractive. But as for if there's anything happening, I haven't seen any signs. Besides, he could have his pick of women. Why would he choose her?"

Krysta didn't recognize the voices and, trapped in the stall as she rearranged her clothing, couldn't see the two women talking. Her Portuguese had improved a lot since her arrival, so she had no problem following the conversation.

The two women went into separate stalls, but continued the conversation.

"Well, you know what they say about what he did to Mariella Guzman—used her for her money and connections, then dumped her. Maybe he thinks the American can help his career."

Letting herself out of the stall, Krysta made her way to the basins. Talk about eavesdroppers hearing no good of themselves!

"I, for one, don't know if I believe that story," the other woman said. "I've worked with Dr. Cisco, and I can't see him doing that to anyone."

After washing her hands, thankfully unable to hear any more of the conversation, Krysta grabbed some hand towels before quickly leaving the room.

She didn't believe that story, either. The man she'd come to know had too much integrity to harm another person in the way it had been rumored, and too much pride to defend himself, probably.

What it did bring to the forefront of her mind, though, was the fact she didn't know the real story. While she'd bared her soul to him, Francisco had held so much of his own life experience back, as though reluctant to share it with her.

Did he not trust her?

That was a sobering thought, and one that made her even more determined to keep their relationship on a casual level.

They'd decided, since all the other visiting specialists were housed at the same apartment building she was in, they would meet instead at Francisco's place. It all took on a sort of cloak-and-dagger aura contrary to her forthright persona, yet made perfect sense in light of the transient nature of their relationship.

No matter how difficult it was to maintain the discretion, she knew she wouldn't change any of it. Coming to Brazil had not only given her a new perspective on the world, but given her a lover for the ages, too. Passionate and masterful, yet gentle and caring.

What more could a woman ask for, especially in her first affair?

Sometimes when she asked herself that, she knew there was an answer she wouldn't want to consider, so she pushed it aside.

She'd put off finding funding for her next project, realizing she needed some time to work on spending time with her family, and getting a life.

As she explained to Francisco, "It doesn't make sense to go back to exactly what I left, when I've realized it wasn't healthy. I'll still be practicing at the hospital, and probably be called in on some outside cases, like the one I assisted with in France, but I'll also have the opportunity to build a more normal life."

He'd nodded and agreed, but something about his closed expression made her wonder what he truly thought, but she didn't want to ask.

There were areas of life they didn't speak about. In particular, what would happen when they parted.

Francisco's accident patient began the long road to recovery, and Krysta had contacted the Belgian company about 3-D printing the orbital floor mesh for the reconstruction. When she explained that Paulista's was considering creating a program where the doctors would be using the virtual surgical mapping and 3-D printing technology, the Belgians were happy to work with her on a price.

"She won't be strong enough for another month or so," she told the company rep. "And I probably won't be in Brazil anymore. But the surgeon handling the case worked with me on the Dos Santos case, and is more than competent to get you all the information you need, as well as perform the surgery."

Enzo Dos Santos was getting ready to leave the hospital soon, too, and although she still had a month before she left, Krysta was starting to feel things coming to an end. At least she still had the clinic trip to Aparecida, and the visit to Francisco's home, to look forward to. Yet, she could feel the time slipping away far more quickly than she'd like, especially when she looked at her calendar and realized she only had one more lecture to give.

It made her stomach feel hollow, empty,

although she knew it would be a new and improved woman going back to New York.

Or would it be?

Somehow, here in Brazil, it seemed easy to change—to get in touch with her femininity, to contemplate a more balanced life. Yet, not even here could she bring herself to make any alterations to her work persona, still fearful doing so would undermine the respect she'd built up.

It all felt as though she were playing a role not really suited for her, and she couldn't help wondering if she were just fooling herself.

She'd always been an outsider, the one who didn't fit in, allowing her to stay safe and unhurt. The outer trappings could change, but had the inner woman truly changed as well?

And what was she risking, spending this time with Francisco?

Impossible to view him as anything but a holiday fling. Despite everything that had happened, she knew there was no future between them. How could there be? They were from different worlds. His experience, in comparison to her lack thereof, must make her seem like nothing more than an amusing diversion.

No, there was nothing serious between them, no matter what emotions she felt when they were together. As he was her first lover, she might be forgiven for thinking there was more to their affair, but as an adult, a woman who thought things through, she knew better. She had to keep that in mind because, although she had no fear of him physically, it would be all too easy to be hurt by him otherwise.

She had to protect herself.

Yet, that night, as she lay in Francisco's arms, she dreaded the moment she'd once more be on her own. Rolling over, she let the last of her inhibitions slip away, so she could make love to him the way she wanted, make him crazy—*louco*—the way he made her every night.

And as she took them both to orgasm, she had to hide her eyes from him, so he wouldn't see her tears.

They drove together to Aparecida, leaving São Paulo at five in the morning to make the drive. Although the clinic organizers had arranged accommodation, Francisco had opted to rent them a room at another venue.

"Aren't you afraid people will talk? After all, they'll know we're staying together."

He shrugged. "It doesn't matter. Any gossip about us will fade quickly."

After you're gone.

He didn't say it, but she heard it in her mind, anyway.

When they arrived at the hospital where the clinic was taking place, Krysta was surprised to see the number of children and adults waiting to be seen or operated on.

Francisco explained, "Often when we have these clinics, parents whose children didn't make the list, or who heard of the clinic too late, will turn up, hoping their child will be seen. The administrators will do the best they can, but it's almost a triage situation at that point. The children with the highest need will get seen if there is time."

It gave her the impetus to work as quickly as she could on the cases she was given, which included two adult cleft-palate repairs. It wasn't something she'd ever seen in the States, where the repairs were generally done on infants, but she'd been forewarned of the cases, and was prepared. Taking a quick break after the second operation, she was walking through the waiting area, on her way outside, when a child and mother caught her attention.

The child was supposed to be feeding, but after every couple of pulls on the mother's breast, the child went limp. When Krysta took a closer look, she could see a blue tinge around the baby's face, and at the ends of the tiny fingers.

Concerned, she approached the mother, and said, in Portuguese, "I am a doctor. May I examine your baby?"

"Sim," she replied, holding out the tiny mite to Krysta, who could hear the relief in the mother's voice.

"What is his name?" she asked, trying to keep the mother calm and engaged as she sat next to her and put the little boy on her lap.

"Paavo," she replied, watching as Krysta opened a package and took out a tongue depressor.

A quick examination confirmed what she suspected, and had her looking around for one of the administrators. When she stood up and caught one's eye, she waved her over. The woman bustled over, looking a little put out.

"This baby should be looked at, preferably by a pediatric surgeon," Krysta said.

"There are only two here today, Doctor," the woman said firmly, in English. "And they are fully booked up. If this lady had applied like the other parents…"

"Whether she did, or she didn't, doesn't matter. This infant needs help. I suspect he has Pierre Robin sequence, and his airway is obstructed each time he tries to feed."

"But…"

Krysta was still holding the baby, keeping him across her arm, his head angled down to allow his airway to remain open. Despite her fragile burden and the mother sitting right there, she was ready to let the other woman have it, when Francisco's calm voice came from behind her.

"Is there a problem here?"

The administrator's attitude and demeanor changed immediately, becoming suddenly sweet. And she reverted to her native language as she replied, "Oh, no. I was just explaining to the American doctor that we have to follow procedure and can't take on patients who weren't preregistered before the rest of the listed patients are seen."

Francisco turned to Krysta, eyebrows raised, and the annoyance she'd felt dealing with the other woman flared a little higher. But she kept her voice cool, almost cold, as she said, in Portuguese, "And I was explaining to the Brazilian administrator that this child has severe glossoptosis, leading to airway obstruction each time he tries to feed. He needs to see a surgeon."

Francisco looked down at the tiny scrap of

a baby lying across her arm and, for an instant, she saw pain flash across his face. Perhaps he was remembering his own brother's problems at that age?

"Pierre Robin sequence, you think?" he asked, looking up at her.

She nodded. "Looks like it. The mandible looks foreshortened, too, although I couldn't be completely sure without a more comprehensive examination."

He turned to the administrator and said, "I will take this case if the pediatric surgeons are too busy."

Then, before the woman could even find her tongue to say anything more, he held out his arms to take the child from Krysta, saying to the child's mother, "Please come with me, so I can examine your baby properly, and then we will see what can be done."

The tears immediately overflowing the mother's eyes, and her obvious gratitude, filled Krysta with satisfaction, and when she put the baby in Francisco's arms and met his gaze, she had a revelation. One she'd been avoiding for, oh, all these many weeks.

This man was one like no other, and she'd fallen for him ass over teakettle, as her granny used to say.

But there was nothing she could do but

try to keep a cool head, and hand the child over. Holding the new knowledge close to her heart, but keeping it off her face and out of her voice, was difficult. She thought she did a credible job when she said, "Thank you."

Then she turned and walked away, back to the one thing she was counting on to keep her sane and give her solace in the future.

Work.

Francisco performed the cleft-palate revision surgery and a tongue-lip adhesion on the infant boy, hopefully giving him the help he needed to begin to grow properly and ultimately thrive. The mother, who lived in a remote area, hours away from Aparecida, had only heard of the clinic two days before. She'd left her home immediately, in hopes of getting her child seen and at least diagnosed.

What the baby really needed was a mandibular distraction osteogenesis, but that operation demanded the child be in the NICU for the entire period needed to lengthen the jaw. There was no hospital near where they lived that could perform the surgery, even if the family could afford it, or have it subsidized. At least with the other two issues dealt with, baby Paavo would have a better chance of survival.

As Francisco washed up after the surgery, he remembered the look on Krysta's face as the administrator had tried to brush her off. He wouldn't be surprised if he hadn't saved the administrator from getting a thorough tongue-lashing. He'd never seen Krysta even slightly ruffled, but at that moment she'd looked ready to go to war.

She was, in every sense of the word, *magnífica*.

He wasn't sure what he was going to do without her.

When she'd told him her next research project had been canceled, he'd felt a brief spurt of hope that perhaps it meant she could stay a little longer in Brazil. But that was just a pipe dream, and he knew it. She was on sabbatical from the hospital, and they would expect her back as soon as her tenure at Paulista's was over.

Really, as much as he wanted to simply enjoy the time they had left together, there was a part of himself already in retreat, trying to salvage whatever he could of pride and heart and soul. Then she goes and does something like going to battle for a tiny baby, one who reminded him so much of João, and he fell in love with her all over again.

Shaking his head at his own folly, he went

to speak to Paavo's mother, making sure to tell her she needed to have the tongue-lip release surgery done the following year. Then it was on to prepare for the next surgery.

They ended up not leaving until after dark, and when they got to their hotel, all they could do was shower and fall into bed, exhausted, hardly saying more than two words to each other the entire time.

Then they woke up the next morning and did it all over again.

"Good job, everyone," Francisco said to the team after the last patient of day two had been taken to recovery. "Thanks to your fine work, we were able to see many more patients than we had originally planned, and the clinic was a great success."

Walking out to the car, Krysta looked as though she were asleep on her feet, but she turned to him and said, "So, where are we going dancing?"

He laughed, shaking his head at her silliness as he opened her door and helped her slip inside. "There'll be time for dancing two nights from now, at my parents' home. All the dancing you want."

She yawned, putting her head back against the headrest. "I'm warning you—I have no idea how to samba, or cha-cha, or merengue, so you may be disappointed."

Leaning on the door, he met her gaze and said, "The cha-cha is Cuban, and the merengue is from the Dominican Republic, so you're okay not knowing those. But the samba? You will learn the samba, even if one of us dies in the effort."

And she was giggling as he shut the door.

It was, he mused, one of the things he loved about her, and being with her. She took her work seriously, but not herself. She had no problem laughing at herself, or just at silly things, and it brought a lightness to his life he'd not known for far too many years.

She made him, his life, better, just by being herself.

Settling into the driver's seat, he said, "Good catch on that baby yesterday. The diagnosis of Pierre Robin sequence was spot-on."

"What were you able to do for him?"

"Tongue-lip adhesion, as well as the cleft-palate repair. Seeing him lying there, prone, in your arms took me back in time."

"Your brother?"

"Mmm, although this little boy today was actually worse off, since João didn't have the glossoptosis. Little Paavo's airway obstruction was severe, and he's in the lowest growth percentile for his age. Hopefully now he can feed without choking on his own tongue, and put on some weight."

"And thank you," she said quietly with a note in her voice he didn't recognize. He glanced at her, but couldn't see anything in the dark interior of the car.

"For what?"

"For taking on the case. For being you."

He wanted to say something in return, but his heart was full, and ached, and it was better to stay silent, rather than say too much.

Not that he should have worried. When he glanced at her at the next stoplight, she was asleep, so that when he whispered, *"Eu te amo,"* it was because he knew she wouldn't hear.

CHAPTER SIXTEEN

KRYSTA AWOKE THE next morning still exhausted, but when she opened her eyes and saw Francisco lying on his side, watching her, she smiled and held out her arms. He'd already warned that they'd be sleeping in separate rooms at his parents, so it would be another couple of nights before they were back in the same bed.

The made love slowly, sweetly, taking their time, finding maximum satisfaction. Having finally admitted to herself that she was in love with Francisco added a new dimension to the experience, and she found herself trying to capture each moment in her memory. It made her stretch out every touch, every kiss, seeking the most she could get out of each one.

"*Amor*, you are torturing me," Francisco groaned.

Torturing herself, too, but in the best possible way.

"Happy birthday," she said, sipping at his skin until he was trembling, goose bumps rising where she touched.

When they achieved orgasm, first her, and then him, her ecstasy was heightened, knowing she'd wrung that deep, pleasure-drunk sound from his throat.

"You know my birthday isn't until tomorrow, don't you?"

"Mmm-hmm. Think of this as an early present."

"Puxa vida," he groaned. "The real gift is going to kill me, isn't it?"

She just laughed softly, and kissed the nipple nearest to her, making it pucker.

After a leisurely breakfast, they left Aparecida and drove south for a short time, before turning west, farther inland. He'd told her it shouldn't take more than a couple of hours to get to his parents' house.

"I was glad to get the offer to work in São Paulo, since it is closer to my parents. Mind you, when I was in Rio they didn't complain half as much about my not visiting, because they knew it was farther to come."

Krysta chuckled. "I have the opposite problem. Since my parents moved to Georgia three years ago, they're constantly complaining that they don't see me, although when they were still in Rochester, they hardly said a word."

They laughed together, and Francisco suggested she take a nap, but she refused. She didn't want to miss any of their time together. She could catch up on sleep in her lonely bed when she got back to New York.

Partway there, he stopped at the side of the road for them to stretch their legs and buy fresh, cold coconuts for them to drink the water.

"This reminds me of the Caribbean," she said, watching the vendor wielding his machete to cut off the top of the husk, then creating a hole in the nut inside.

When he handed her the coconut, he also tried to give her a straw, which she declined, telling him, "I'm sure I remember how to drink these the way my grandfather taught me." And thankfully she did, getting the cool fresh liquid from the coconut into her mouth, rather than down her chin and the front of her blouse.

"Brava! Brava!" the vendor cried, the two of them laughing together.

She took that spirit of fun with her for the rest of the journey, determined to enjoy the trip. When they pulled up at Francisco's parents' home, she got out of the car and stretched, just as the door flew open and what seemed like a battalion of people spilled out, all seemingly talking at the same time. They engulfed the car, Francisco and, to her surprise, Krysta, too.

It was a whirl of names and faces as she was grabbed and kissed on both cheeks by everyone. Not knowing what to expect, it was a little overwhelming, but she smiled and tried to remember who was who in the crowd.

Finally, Francisco's mother shooed everyone back inside. "Let them breathe. Let them breathe. João, take Krysta's bag into the house. Your brother's, too."

"I believe he's quite capable of carrying his own bag," was João's saucy reply. "Irrespective of him being so very old now."

That led to a mock wrestling match, with fake blows thrown, and some trash talking. This was a Francisco she'd never seen before, although the ghost of it came out sometimes when they spoke and laughed. Relaxed, teasing and being teased. Just a part of a family that obviously shared great love and respect.

"Ah, boys," Senhora Carvalho said with a smile as she tucked her arm through Krysta's and pulled her toward the door. "They can be doctors and architects, but a part of them never truly grows up."

The house was large and rambling, but smelled wonderfully of good food, and sounded like a family home should—ringing with laughter and teasing remarks shouted down corridors.

"You're in here with me," Francisco's youngest sister, Teresa, said, leading the way down the hallway. Raising her voice, she added, "Because although Mathile has the biggest room, she takes up more space than I do!"

"You would as well, if you were eight months pregnant," came the shouted reply, and Krysta exchanged a laughing look with Teresa.

Even as she tried to be as unobtrusive as possible, neither Francisco nor the rest of his family would allow it, pulling her into conversations, slowing their speech when they realized her Portuguese may not be up to the rapid-fire quips and barbs flying around.

Although the *festa* in honor of Francisco's birthday wasn't until the following day, everyone seemed in a party mood already, and his mother had cooked a feast of a dinner.

"Take Krysta and show her the animals," Francisco's father suggested, and she was glad of a small reprieve from the noise and crowd.

Senhor Carvalho had a small farm, which augmented his salary as a water-quality inspector for the area, Francisco explained, but he thought the real reason for the farm was that his father loved animals. There were at least three dogs underfoot in the house, and a cat that stayed up on a high shelf in the living room, surveying the surroundings with feline superiority.

Now Krysta found herself meeting chickens and ducks, a large sow and a donkey that was far friendlier than any she'd met before.

"The last donkey I came in contact with tried to take a chunk out of me," she said, smiling up at Francisco while scratching the donkey's muzzle. "This one is sweet."

Another cat slunk out of the barn, giving them a disdainful glance before disappearing into the nearby bushes.

"Mama said she has kittens in the barn. Want to look?" he asked.

Of course she did, and they found the four little wriggling fluff balls in a disused stall, their eyes not even open yet.

"How darling," she crooned, stroking them lightly with her forefinger. "So soft."

When she stood up, she found Francisco

barring her way to the door, and it seemed the most natural thing in the world to go into his arms, and exchange a long, drugging kiss.

After she'd seen the vegetable garden and coffee trees, it was back inside to clean up for dinner, which was served on the courtyard at the back of the house.

Since she hadn't contributed to fixing the meal, Krysta offered to help with the cleanup, and found herself absorbed into a laughing, chattering swirl of women. At first she didn't notice, and then she realized they were determined to winkle any information about her relationship with Francisco out of her, by hook or by crook. But she was used to keeping her own counsel and deflected the interrogation as best she could.

Yes, she thought him very nice.

No, they were work colleagues and friends, and he'd wanted her to see as much of Brazil as she could before she left.

It was like being in a sword fight, she thought as the last dish was washed and put away, but with multiple opponents all coming at you at the same time, and it was a relief to escape back outside, where the conversation was more general.

She went to bed with a wave to everyone, being careful not to single out Francisco in any discernible way, and, not surprisingly, she fell asleep as soon as her head hit the pillow.

The day of the party was another whirl of activity, and the preparations made the time fly. Before she knew it, it was time to change, and the music was already beginning outside.

If it had seemed like there was a mass of people with just the family there, now it was a crush. The party spread out from the house to the courtyard, and beyond. She was taken around and introduced to so many people her head was spinning, and her usually good memory all but deserted her.

Just before dinner was served, she found herself standing with Francisco and his other brother, Antonio, the latter taking her hand and kissing it lightly.

"I don't think you will want to be with this old man anymore," he teased. "Not now that you've met his younger, more handsome brother."

Francisco rolled his eyes, and smacked his brother on the back of the head. "Why don't you go try out your smooth lines on some of the little girls making eyes at you? They will probably appreciate them more."

"*Oi!* Watch the hair," was the testy answer.

"Come and dance with me," Francisco

said, insisting when she demurred, saying she should go and help his mother in the kitchen. "She has five hundred women in there already," was his reply. "She won't even miss you."

But it wasn't that she wanted to be in the kitchen, or even that she didn't know the steps. It was knowing being in his arms, even for a dance lesson, would be the ultimate in pleasure-filled pain. Especially since they were trying not to let his family know what lay between them.

Yet still, she gave in, unable to resist.

"Since it's your birthday," she said, infusing her voice with disgruntlement.

He just laughed, and led her to where some of the partygoers were already making use of the dance floor.

To her surprise, she caught on to the steps fairly quickly, although cognizant of the fact he kept it simple for her, not expecting her to do any of the fancier footwork going on around them. And she enjoyed it, finding herself laughing with delight, loving the way the swaying lanterns above their heads cast intriguing shadows on his face, and how easily he laughed with her.

It was a night to remember, and as the party wound down, Krysta found herself beside Senhora Carvalho, who had finally decided she'd done everything necessary and could sit for a moment. Francisco was dancing with a lovely blonde woman he'd introduced as his cousin, and they were putting on a show. It was beautiful to watch.

"My Francisco is a good dancer, isn't he? I think it's important that a man know how to move to music."

"Yes, he is," Krysta agreed, trying to tear her gaze away from him and having a hard time of it.

"But even more important," her companion went on, "is that he is a good man."

Krysta turned to find the older woman watching her, not the dancing, and schooled her own face to stillness. "Yes, he is," she agreed again.

"He was hurt, very badly, by people he thought friends, by a woman he held dear. I would hate to see that happen again. He deserves better. Just as I believe you do, too."

"Yes," Krysta said again, sadness washing through her, her gaze drawn back to where Francisco undulated, his feet flying faster than she could follow.

It was a warning his mother offered, obviously not fooled by their attempt to seem to be only friends. But it was a warning that, for Krysta, had come far too late.

As always, Francisco enjoyed his time with his family, but he was eager to get back to São Paulo, not for work, but to have Krysta to himself again. The time was ticking away, even swifter now than ever.

He listed what was yet to come in his head, trying to take comfort in the fact none of them had yet occurred.

One more of her lectures.

A postoperative checkup of Enzo Dos Santos.

A conference call with the manufacturers in Belgium, so she could guide him and the rest of the team through the steps they'd need to take to work with the company.

The farewell dinner, back at the place where it started. A circle closing that he wished could turn into a Möbius strip, so it never had to end.

These were the landmarks he would use to mark the final days with her, and as hard as he tried to not think about them, the more they weighed on his mind.

It didn't help that she was unusually quiet on the drive back, seemingly sunk deep in thought. When he questioned her, she just shook her head, sending him a little smile.

"I'm just tired. It's been a hectic few days."

With that he could definitely agree, but then he knew he was in trouble when she asked to be dropped at her apartment, rather than coming home with him.

He wanted to beg, and the impulse angered him, so he just agreed, without asking why, or trying to discover what was wrong.

Yet, there was one thing he absolutely had to know. So, as he pulled into the parking lot outside the apartment building, he turned to her and asked, "Did someone in my family, or at the party, say something to upset you? Did I do something?"

"No," she said. "They were all lovely. You know they were. And so were you."

But she wasn't looking at him when she said it, searching her handbag instead, coming out with her keys.

Self-preservation insisted he not push, so he got out to open her door, and walked her into the lobby, wheeling her bag behind him.

Should he kiss her good-night? He didn't know, couldn't read this new mood she was in.

"Até logo," she said, reaching up to kiss him on his cheeks, as though they were noth-

ing more than the friends they'd pretended to be at his parents' house. "See you tomorrow."

Then she took her bag from his suddenly nerveless grip, and stepped into the elevator. But although she tried not to show any emotion, she kept her gaze on his until the doors closed, and he could have sworn there was deep pain glimmering in her eyes.

CHAPTER SEVENTEEN

KRYSTA LET HERSELF into her apartment and deflated like a popped balloon. She felt like an idiot, a coward. She should have spoken to Francisco, at least made an attempt to tell him what she was feeling, and why she was so distant, but she didn't feel equipped to do it right now. There was a tender, hurting space around her heart that didn't feel as though it could take any more blows.

She'd tried to call on the old Krysta—prosaic, practical Krysta—to come up with a solution to her conundrum, but unfortunately that woman seemed to have taken a holiday, at the worst possible time.

So she had no answers to the question she kept asking herself, over and over again.

Which would be better, less painful, for both herself and Francisco: Break it off now, or see it through to the end?

Leaving her bags by the door, she wandered into the apartment, and sat down on the couch. The memories of their first night together tried to intrude, but she pushed them back. If she thought about him in a sexual way, she'd never work it all out. Besides, it was no longer about just physical satisfaction, at least not for her.

When they were together, she felt lighter, better, freer, than she ever had before. He'd helped her become stronger. She'd always been confident in her abilities as a doctor and surgeon. That had never been in question. But as a woman? She'd known she was lacking. It was why her work became her be-all and end-all. If you don't put yourself out there, you don't have to try to figure things out. You can just drift along, secure in your little space.

And now, hurt and confused, as much as it was tempting to retreat back into that little space, she knew she'd no longer fit in it. She'd grown in ways she'd never imagined she could, and there was a part of her eager to keep growing, but right now it felt as if without Francisco she might not be able to.

A foolish notion, she was sure. There were few things she'd set her mind to that she hadn't been able to achieve, and she was determined to rebuild her familial relationships, expand her horizons and keep moving forward in life.

She could do that, without anyone's help.

But she would love to have Francisco beside her, encouraging her, stretching her when she'd be tempted to lapse back into her old ways.

That, too, was just a dream. Nothing had changed from the first night they'd been together when she'd so boldly, so foolishly, thumbed her nose at love. They would still be going their separate ways, his life here in Brazil, hers in America.

No, nothing had changed, except her feelings for him, which had grown and expanded until they seemed to inhabit every corner of her being. How was she to know he'd fill her so completely, so thoroughly, the thought of being without him created a physical ache?

Yet, there was also more than just the divide caused by their work lives to consider. For all the time they'd spent together, Francisco still held a part of himself in abeyance. Not physically, but in other ways. He'd never talked about what happened between him and his ex-fiancée, or even much about his modeling career. Not that it was terribly important, just that it seemed to show he didn't totally trust her, nor did he want to allow her access to the deepest parts of his heart.

She wished she had the courage to simply ask him, to demand that of him, but she didn't. To do so and be rejected would hurt even more than his reticence. He'd have to volunteer the information himself, and without that openness, she knew there couldn't be a long-term relationship between them.

But for all that, she'd hurt him this evening. It had been plain on his face, and considering all they'd shared, the way she'd handled it was unforgivable. She'd definitely lapsed into old, selfish ways, where the only person she'd had to think of was herself, and that was *all* she'd thought of.

Like his mother said, he deserved better, and although she couldn't be his forever, the least she could do was be better now. After rummaging through her bag, she found her phone, and called him. Even texting would be cowardly tonight, and she was determined to do the right thing.

He answered immediately, traffic noise in the distance telling her he hadn't got home yet.

"Oi," he said, and hearing the caution in his voice made her ache even more.

"I'm sorry. I behaved like a child, running away."

There was a little silence, and her heart raced with fear and self-recrimination. When he spoke, his voice was softer, and her eyes prickled with tears.

"What were you running away from, *amor*?"

"Myself. My feelings. My fears."

He sighed, a long, hard exhale. "I understand. Sometimes it's easier than facing them, yes?"

"Definitely," she agreed. "Especially when you don't know the right thing to do."

"I don't know, either."

"I'm so confused, Francisco."

There was another pause while he thought. It was one of the many things she loved about him: the careful consideration he gave decisions. When he spoke again, there was a tone in his voice she didn't recognize.

"Forget right or wrong at this moment. What do you *want* to do?"

That was easy. "Be with you."

"Then come back downstairs, or I will come upstairs, and we will spend tonight together. Tomorrow is soon enough to try to find the answers."

"How soon will you get here?" she asked, her heart thumping now with joy, fear fleeing at the thought of even one more moment with him.

"I never left. Like a lovelorn young boy, I have been sitting in the parking lot, wondering what next to do. How I can make right whatever I did to wrong you."

She should laugh, but the air was stuck in her lungs, and the tears had made a lump form in her throat. Swallowing it hurt, as though the lump was mixed with shards of glass, destined to lacerate her heart. But she forced it down and, wanting to be where they'd spent so many beautiful nights together, said, "I'll be right there."

They drove silently to his place, going inside still without speaking. There was a sense that what there was between them had grown fragile and words might cause it to break into a million, irredeemable pieces.

Any questions to be asked and answered tonight were posed through looks, and touches.

Do you want to make love with me?

He asked with fingers spanning her wrist, his thumb moving gently against the pulse point. Although the only point of contact, she felt it down to her toes.

Yes.

She answered with a kiss, set against the

side of his mouth, gentle and tempting, but not demanding. Then she walked into his bedroom, leading him, despite the fact it was he who held her.

They made love slowly, almost carefully, until the passion overtook them, and thought fled, leaving just sensation. His mouth on her. His hands. His skin beneath her fingertips and palms. The hard length of him filling her, taking her to ecstasy.

Grateful for the surcease from conflicted emotion, she rode the waves with him, feeling the moment he, too, let go, and they could fly together.

Drifting into sleep, she held on to that, letting the memory lull her, wishing she could hold on to it—to him—forever.

Francisco woke first, and turned his head to watch Krysta sleep.

Despite the beauty of the night just spent with her, he ached. Not physically. That would be bearable. No, this was deeper, harder to heal.

He'd thought he'd known what heartbreak was. Had known what love was. But looking at the woman beside him, he realized what he'd felt before had been an illusion. The emotions of a young man, still inexperienced and susceptible to the lure of a pretty face and the right words.

And he knew the heartbreak coming would be devastating.

He'd known the relationship with her wouldn't last, but still he had dreamed.

Had acknowledged to himself that, as her first lover, it was assured she would move on, find others. Hopefully she would think of him fondly and, should they meet at a conference or seminar, share with him a smile redolent of good memories.

But there, too, he'd dreamed—of being her first, her last. Of being enough that she would never want another.

Foolish to dream. He wasn't in the dreaming business. Medicine demanded logic, foresight, patience, determination. Those were qualities he'd cultivated, but none of them had stopped him from giving his heart where it wasn't safe. From loving more than was wise.

Yet, there was a little sense of having failed her—them—in the way he held parts of himself back. He hadn't found the courage to open himself up completely to her, to put himself on the line, and ask her to stay.

Theirs would be the kind of love story without a happy ending, and he couldn't lay bare his heart to her, knowing she would walk away.

Krysta stirred, as though hearing his thoughts in her dreams, and when her eyes opened, he thought he might drown in the emotion swirling in them.

"I know I said I wouldn't, and I didn't want to, but I've fallen in love with you."

She spoke softly, in her habitual matter-of-fact way, and for a moment his heart leaped with joy. If they loved, truly, deeply, they could find a way, couldn't they? But before he could voice that thought, she continued.

"Besides that, nothing in our circumstances has changed. I'll be going back to New York in two weeks. You've built a life for yourself here, in a place that you love, where you belong. I wish I could say I would give everything I've worked for up for you, but I can't. I know I'll resent it and, eventually, you. I've changed a lot since I came here, but not enough to throw my life's work away."

And he knew then what the right words were. Not what he'd been thinking, for they were born of dreams, not reality.

"And I would never ask you to. You've done great things, and there is so much more you have to contribute. To even consider asking you to give that up would be sacrilege."

They both knew Brazil could offer her nothing like what she already had, and despite the connectivity of the world, eventually she would start to fall behind.

As for him, he didn't know how to get around the thought that perhaps she only believed herself in love with him, because he was her first love affair. Only too well did he remember how all-encompassing those emotions could be, and how they could, in reality, be false.

"What do you want to do?" Her voice trembled, and he knew she was fighting tears. Her eyes glistened with them. "Do you want us to stop seeing each other now?"

"Will that make our parting any less painful?" he asked, knowing for him it wouldn't.

"No." She shook her head, lifted her hand to dash away the tears spilling down her cheeks. "No, it won't."

"Then let us enjoy each other until the very last moment. There will be time enough to mourn this beautiful thing we created, later."

And he still believed that, even as the days rushed, one into the other, and their lovemaking became increasingly frantic, as the nights fled by, too.

He heard from Flávia, and told Krysta he'd arranged for a tour of the sanctuary.

"Will you be coming, too?" she asked.

"If you promise to keep me safe from spiders," he said, making her chuckle, as he intended.

So they went, and although it wasn't anywhere he'd rush back to, it had been informative, and Krysta had seemed to know just the right questions to ask.

At the end, Flávia had hugged her, and asked, "Can we keep in touch? I do like you."

"Of course," Krysta replied. "I don't know when next I'll be coming this way, but if you're ever in the States, no matter where, let me know."

The new Krysta, he believed, would keep that promise, and perhaps the two often-isolated women would remain friends.

Her last lecture came and went, and his pride knew no bounds at her poise beforehand, so different from that first day when she'd had to throw up. And he'd clapped harder than anyone during the standing ovation at the end.

The time for Enzo Dos Santos's last checkup with her arrived, and they both forced a laugh when Enzo said to Francisco, "I still prefer her, over you, but I suppose you will have to do."

"Your recovery is remarkable," she told

him, obviously pleased at his progress, especially in regard to his speech therapy. "And I'll be checking on you from afar, so make sure you behave."

He'd sketched her a salute, making her laugh again, and then that milestone, too, was past.

And then, suddenly, far too soon, there were just two days left before she was to leave.

He took her back to Santos, and this time he braved the water with her. Taking her to the beach where the surfers hung out, he rented wet suits and boards, and taught her to surf in the relatively gentle waves. Why he'd thought of it, he wasn't sure. Perhaps because he wanted to give her one more reminder of how much she'd changed. One more proof of her courage.

She was surprised at how well she did, but he wasn't. There was an indomitable spirit within her that, along with her intellect, would assure her success in whatever she turned her mind to.

It was something he believed with all his heart, and he told her so.

When her face lit up with pleasure at his words, his heart broke just a little more at how beautiful she was when that inner light shone out from her soul through her eyes.

One more walk on the beach, another coffee. Dinner at the outdoor restaurant they had been to before. A kiss beneath the moonlight on their way to the car.

All these things he stored in his memory, wishing they could go on forever.

Then the second to last day was done.

And he still hadn't confessed his own feelings to her, just held them close to his breaking heart.

CHAPTER EIGHTEEN

THE CLOSING RECEPTION passed in a blur. Throughout the dinner, speeches and schmoozing, all Krysta could do was wonder where the time had gone.

Hadn't she blinked, and the months flew by?

The last weeks with Francisco, in particular, had gone by in a flash, and even though they'd made their decision, agreed on how their affair should play out, there was a part of her that refused to believe it was about to be over.

Yet, what did she know about love, really? How could she know whether in a week, or a month, or a year, she'd wouldn't stop yearning for him? That the memory of his smile, his kiss, his touch, wouldn't fade into insignificance?

And despite the beauty of his lovemaking, the way he looked at her, especially when he didn't think she'd see, Francisco hadn't actually told her how he felt about her or their relationship, still holding an integral part of himself locked away. It made her think she was doing the right thing, even as she desperately wanted to hold on to him, however possible.

It was a fight with no winners. A riddle with no answer.

It was their last night together. She'd packed all her things and moved them to his apartment, so they could go straight there from the closing reception. They'd been quiet with each other, perhaps each making a defensive retreat in the face of the parting ahead. In Santos they'd talked and talked, as though to fit in a lifetime of stories into one sun-drenched day. And they'd laughed, even though there was already a painful edge to their amusement.

At the reception, she saw Dr. Delgado glaring across the room at them, and couldn't help asking, "Why does that man dislike you so much?"

Francisco's lips tightened, and then he relaxed, and sighed.

"He is a distant cousin to the young woman I was engaged to, and is determined to think the worst of me."

"Just shows how little he knows you," she said as casually as she could, knowing this was probably her last chance to hear his side of the story. "I've heard the rumors. What really happened?"

The look he gave her scorched her to her toes, and for an instant he looked as though he wanted to kiss her, right there, in front of everyone.

"You are the first person to ask me that," he said, his voice low and rough. "Most just assume what they read or heard was true."

She kept her gaze level, wanting him to know she meant it when she replied, "Then obviously they're not particularly good judges of character. I think you'd find there are a number of people in the hospital who don't believe the stories, either."

His gaze was so intent, as he searched her face, she felt it like a physical touch. Then he took her hand and led her to the side of the room, where they wouldn't be overheard.

"I fell for Mari when we were both models. The difference between us was that she came from a wealthy family, and, well, my family was much poorer than it is now. Our upbringings were worlds apart, but I thought we had something special, and between the money I'd saved from modeling and what I'd make as a doctor, we'd have a good life. I asked her to marry me, and she agreed, but then I found out she was hooked on cocaine, and told her I couldn't marry her unless she got clean."

He shook his head, a rueful smile tugging at one corner of his lips.

"She left me, after taking most of my money, apparently wanting the drugs more than she wanted me. But she couldn't let anyone know why things had ended between us. So, she and her friends began telling everyone that I had deserted her, and when her father found out she was using, she told him she had only started because of the breakup. By then, I had just finished medical school, and the general consensus was that I had used her, and her wealth, to get what I wanted and then discarded her."

"I'm sorry." She touched his wrist in sympathy, but inside she was shaken and angry on his behalf. No one deserved to be treated that way, least of all Francisco, who was so proud, and had so much integrity. "Addiction is a disease that makes people do things the rest of us can't understand."

"Sim," he replied, the warmth in his eyes melting her heart. "Thank you."

"For what?" she asked.

"For believing in me, even when you didn't know the whole story."

Walking into the apartment after the reception, she paused, took a deep breath. In these rooms she'd spent the happiest days of her life, and had discovered herself in a way she couldn't have done on her own. Turning to him, she wanted to tell him that, make him understand she'd never forget him, never be ungrateful for the time they'd spent together, but there was something in his eyes that stilled the words on her tongue.

"Come to bed, *amor*." He held out his hand and, without reservation, she laid hers in it. "I don't want to talk anymore. I want only to feel."

They made love far into the night, and he didn't say anything when, as she lay above him, her tears fell on his face. Instead, he just held her tighter, and kissed them away, making her wish with all her heart that he could love her, too, the way she loved him.

The next morning, he drove her to the airport, although Paulista's had offered a limo to take her. A part of her thought they should have said their goodbyes at his home, but the bigger part still was greedy, demanding every last moment she could have with him.

She checked in, and afterward they looked

at each other, neither wanting to suggest she go through security, both knowing she should.

They walked slowly to the security barrier, and stood, hand in hand, watching the crowds. Needing one last point of contact, one last memory, she turned, and found his gaze trained on her face, a look of such longing in his eyes it made her heart clench, the pain making her gasp.

Then she was in his arms, his face in her neck, her tears dampening the front of his shirt.

"Eu te amo," he said. *"Eu te amarei para sempre."*

She froze, her brain scrambling to understand, to accept what he was saying. Desperate thoughts ran through her mind, about staying, asking him to come with her, as, at that moment, she knew she would love him forever, too.

Then common sense took over. He was playing their affair out to the end, with the perfect goodbye to put a period on their time together. If that were not the case, wouldn't he have said something earlier, rather than wait until now, when there was no more time to talk, to negotiate?

So, although there was so much she wanted

to say, to ask, to tell him, all she whispered was, "I love you, too, Francisco."

And then she forced herself to walk away, uncaring of the stares her tearstained cheeks garnered her.

Rochester seemed flat and bland after the colors of Brazil, but she threw herself back into work, trying to regain the momentum she'd had before she left. Yet, she really wasn't the same, and the cutthroat world of applying and securing grants didn't hold the same appeal as before.

Without the new research project, she had some time on her hands, and used it to visit first her parents, and then her older brother, his wife and two kids. Sitting in Kelvin's backyard, in Houston, he finally broached the subject of the change in her.

"Mom told me not to ask, but I have to," he said. "What happened in Brazil? You're a different person. You even look different."

Even after a month, the thought of Francisco brought tears to her eyes, and she looked away, so he wouldn't see.

"You can tell me," he said quietly, putting his hand on her arm. "Whatever it was couldn't have been a totally bad thing."

"I was a wonderful thing," she said, sniffling. "His name is Francisco."

"Wait, what?" Kelvin leaned forward, searching her eyes. "What the hell… You fell in love! So where is he, and when do we get to meet him?" Then his eyes narrowed. "Or do I have to fly to Brazil and beat the crap out of him?"

That made her laugh, as he knew it would.

"No, you don't have to beat him up. The reality is, I'm here and he's there, and our jobs don't leave us much option to be together. We decided it would be better to just end it, rather than torture ourselves until it fizzled out."

Kelvin was an engineer, with the kind of mind that cut through the nonsense to the meat of any problem. So, she wasn't too surprised when he said, "Does it feel like it's fizzling out?"

"No, it doesn't. In fact, it hurts a little more every day."

He leaned back, and took a long swig of his beer.

"I think you should find a way to be together. Love doesn't come along every day, especially not for people like us."

She knew what he meant. They were both driven and hyperfocused, sometimes unable to see past whatever they were concentrating on. Somehow Ginny, his wife, had gotten through to him, and they'd been happily married for over six years.

Could she hope for a similar happy outcome? She highly doubted it.

Yet, even through her misery, her brain kept cycling back to that moment at the airport, when Francisco said he'd love her forever. She'd attributed it to a whim on his part to make their affair end as romantically as it had played out, but was that really the type of man Francisco was?

No.

His integrity would never allow him to say something as monumental as that if he didn't mean it.

And yet, she'd walked away, rather than gather her courage and try to work it out.

Was it too late for them?

"Put your mind to it," Kelvin said. "If anyone can find a solution, it's you."

Francisco let himself into his apartment, and hung his keys on the hook by the door. Then he inhaled, deeply. Although it had been over a month since Krysta left, every time he came home, he swore he could still smell her distinctive fresh scent in the air.

He didn't know whether that made him

insane, but if he wasn't there yet, he soon would be.

Missing her was a constant ache, so much so he'd realized he couldn't go on this way. Soon his work would suffer, and Delgado was still making snide remarks, going so far as to question his abilities. One slip, and he knew he'd be out. Delgado would see to it.

Before he'd met Krysta that would have made him incensed, but losing her had made him realize there were far more important things than work, or his pride, or even opening himself up to pain. Looking back, he could no longer understand the reasons he'd used for letting her go. Now they seemed flimsy, rather than anything important.

He'd refused to allow them the chance they deserved, because he was afraid it would all turn to dust. Yet, deep inside, he knew what they'd shared was extraordinary—a once in a lifetime connection. One that he'd foolishly thrown away out of fear.

Moving to the sofa, he threw himself down on it.

Today he'd given in to his craving for her, and tried to call, but couldn't get through. Her cell phone had gone to voice mail, and the hospital in Rochester had said she was away.

They wouldn't give out any further information. He'd left a message, asking her to call.

Maybe she was visiting her parents. He hoped, wherever she was, she was having a good time. Trying something new. Living her best life.

Even if it were without him.

She'd said she loved him, but when he'd finally admitted he loved her, too, she'd walked away. He knew it was because he'd left it too late, had agreed with her when she'd said nothing had changed about their lives.

Everything had changed for him. Meeting her, loving her, had caused the kind of seismic emotional shift only love can. There was the knowledge he'd give anything, do anything, to be with her again.

Life was too short to waste any more of it on wondering whether they could make it together or not. If he couldn't contact her by phone, he would go and find her, ask her to take him for her own, for as long as she might want him, in whatever capacity she wanted.

He was so lost in thought when his phone rang it startled him. Not even looking at the screen, he clicked it on while lifting it to his ear.

"*Oi.*" There was a pause, and he almost hung up.

"Francisco?"

Joy, unfettered and complete, fired through him, and he found himself on his feet.

"Krysta? *Amor*?"

"Yes."

The joy he felt echoed back at him from her voice, and his heart began to race.

"Where are you?"

She didn't reply, just asked, "Am I still your *amor*? Do you still love me?"

"Yes. And yes. I ache for you. I don't want to live without you anymore."

He heard her gasp, and then he heard a sniffle. Was she crying?

"Don't cry, *amor*. I can't bear it if you cry and I am not there to wipe your tears."

"Then let me in, darling. I'm outside."

For an instant he thought she was joking, but he knew she would never be so cruel. And when, in a matter of minutes, she was in his arms, he swore he would never let her go again.

He couldn't stop kissing her, touching her, his hands and lips seeking to make sure she was actually there, and not a figment of his love-crazed imagination.

When they finally came up for breath, he asked, "When did you arrive? Why didn't you let me know you were coming?"

"I flew in today, and it was only when I was in the air I realized you might not even be here." She shook her head, a smile tilting her lips. "I wasn't thinking straight. You know how I am. I get an idea and run with it, full speed ahead. I wanted to tell you something, but face-to-face, not on the phone."

"Tell me," he said. "And then I will tell you mine."

"I don't want to be apart from you anymore, so I'm thinking of leaving the hospital in Rochester after my contract is up, and the French transplant team has offered me a job. I know it's asking a lot, but you said you love Paris, and the Belgians are looking for a representative in France—someone to demonstrate the products, hands-on—if you think you might be interested—"

"Yes," he said before she could finish. Then kissed her again to seal the deal. "Yes. And yes. And yes."

"Oh, Francisco. *Eu te amarei para sempre.*"

Heart soaring, he picked her up and, carrying her to his bedroom, he echoed her words. "And I will love you, forever."

"What was your news?" she asked as he laid her down on his bed, and came to rest above her.

"I was going to tell you that I will go anywhere with you, and be happy, as long as I am by your side. I planned to go to Rochester to tell you in person, but you beat me to it."

"You snooze, you lose, my love."

She grinned up at him, and he bent to kiss the smile off her lips, but paused with their mouths millimeters apart, to say, "No, *amor*. In this case, we both win."

* * * * *

Look out for the next story in the
A Summer in São Paulo trilogy

Falling for the Single Dad Surgeon
by Charlotte Hawkes

And there is another fabulous
story to come!
Available June 2020

If you enjoyed this story, check out
these other great reads from
Ann McIntosh

The Nurse's Christmas Temptation
Surgeon Prince, Cinderella Bride
The Surgeon's One Night to Forever
The Nurse's Pregnancy Miracle

All available now!